CONDORMAN

**Walt Disney Productions
presents**

CONDORMAN

book by
Joe Claro

Based on the Screenplay by
Marc Stirdivant

Directed by
Charles Jarrott

SCHOLASTIC BOOK SERVICES
NEW YORK · TORONTO · LONDON · AUCKLAND · SYDNEY · TOKYO

To
Chris, Danielle, Nöel,
Nicole, and Natasha

ISBN 0-590-32022-X

12 11 10 9 8 7 6 5 4 3   1 2 3 4 5 6/8

Harry Oslo stood in the middle of the large, tree-lined park. He craned his neck and looked up to the top of the Eiffel Tower.

A lot of other people were doing the same thing, but they were tourists. The tower was one of the things they'd come to Paris to see.

Harry lived in Paris. He'd been working at the U.S. embassy in France for a year. He could see the Eiffel Tower whenever he looked out his office window.

So Harry wasn't sightseeing. He was helping with an experiment. The camera around his neck and the walkie-talkie in his hands were his equipment. They belonged to the man sitting near the top of the tower.

Almost a thousand feet above Harry's head,

Woody Wilkins sat dangling his legs over the side of a ledge. He wore a skintight jumpsuit that was covered with feathers. Each of his arms was strapped to some kind of contraption — about the size of a door.

Harry walked to a prearranged spot and switched on his walkie-talkie. Still looking upward, he spoke into the mouthpiece.

"Okay, Woody," he said. "I'm in position."

Harry's walkie-talkie crackled. Then he heard his friend's voice.

"Get ready!" Woody ordered.

Harry got down on one knee and pointed the camera. Through the telephoto lens, he could see Woody adjusting his throat mike. As he aimed the camera, he heard Woody recite through the walkie-talkie:

"Who can save the Princess Juliet from the evil Count Lorca? Who can save the city? Who? Who? This is a job for — CONDOR-MAN!"

Woody was on his feet now. Harry began snapping pictures as Woody stepped off the ledge. He extended his arms in one smooth motion, and the planks at his sides opened out. They were painted to match the feathers that covered Woody's jumpsuit.

With a wingspan of fifteen feet, Condorman

sailed out over the square. Harry snapped away like crazy. Everyone else stared up at the crazy man in the weird hang glider.

Woody shifted his wings, dipping and soaring with the light wind. The laughter and cheers of the crowd rose to him from the square. And through it all, Harry kept taking pictures.

Suddenly, there was a loud crack! One of the wings folded in half. Woody began flapping like a bird. The condor began to behave like a dodo.

"Oh, no!" Harry screamed. "Flap, Woody, flap!"

Woody began to spiral off into the distance, losing altitude all the time. Harry followed, but there was no way he could keep up with the plummeting Condorman.

Harry was still running when he heard the splash. That was a good sign. If Woody had fallen into the Seine he had a chance of survival.

Harry raced down a maze of side streets, following a shortcut to the river. He hopped over a railing onto a small bridge. The camera around his neck sailed behind him, caught up, and hit him in the ear.

He didn't even feel the pain because he saw

his friend, still alive, thrashing in the water.

"Swim, Woody, swim!"

"Harryyyyyyyyyyyyyyy!"

"I'm coming!" Harry screamed. He kicked off his shoes, dropped the camera and the walkie-talkie, and bounded into the water feet first. Then he splashed his way toward Woody.

"Try not to swallow, Woody! Keep your beak closed!"

Harry reached his friend and managed to loosen the straps on his arms. The wings floated away as Harry dragged Woody toward the bank.

Some onlookers helped him pull the soggy birdman to dry land and watched as Harry bent down to give artificial respiration. When Woody began breathing again, Harry sat up and looked around at the crowd that had formed.

"He's okay," he said to no one in particular. "He...he's a friend of mine. Endangered species. He's...well, he's a nut."

"Harry," Woody said weakly.

"Don't talk, Woody. Try to breathe first."

"Harry," Woody gasped. "How did it look? I mean before it broke? Did you get the pictures?"

"What are you talking about?" Harry screamed. "You nearly drowned!"

"Did you get the pictures?"

"Yeah, yeah, I got the pictures," Harry said, standing over Woody. "You looked great."

"Don't lie to me, Harry," Woody moaned. "We both know the truth. Condorman is in serious trouble!"

After Woody passed out, Harry got some of the onlookers to help get him into a cab. Then the doorman at Harry's building helped get the would-be bird up to Harry's apartment. Recovered now, Woody sat hunched over his drawing table, a blanket around his shoulders, his feet soaking in a large basin of hot water.

Woody's table, together with all his other art equipment, had been set up in a corner of Harry's living room. Harry had invited Woody to stay with him while he was visiting Paris for the purposes of the Condorman experiment.

Harry came out of his kitchen carrying a cup of hot tea. Woody was staring at his drawings. He seemed to be in a trance, until an explosive sneeze carried him back.

"I don't understand it," Woody mumbled. "It should have worked."

"Drink this, Woody. It'll help." Woody stared at the steaming tea. "Just sip it slowly, and calm down."

"I AM CALM!" Woody yelled. Then he lowered his voice. "I mean, I am calm. The wings were foolproof. They should have worked."

Harry put the tea on the table in front of Woody. "Woody," he said, "you're a great cartoonist. You're a great comic book writer. It's just that you're a lousy bird. You could have killed yourself."

"Harry," Woody said, throwing the blanket from his shoulders, "that's the way I create. You know that. If I can't do something in real life, I won't have Condorman do it in my comics."

Excited, he started to stand up, then remembered where his feet were, and settled for gesturing, instead of pacing the floor.

"Kids all over the world read my stuff. They trust me! They *know* if I'm faking it. Condorman is an American! His word is his bond!"

"Hooray for the red, white, and blue!" Harry said, reaching out to steady the rocking tea cup in front of Woody. "We've been buddies for a long time, Woody. I admire you. You're sincere. You're conscientious. But sometimes I think you carry things too far."

"How so?" Woody asked, sitting back in his

chair. He seemed truly surprised at his friend's observation.

"Well," Harry said, "take now, for instance. Condorman's assignment is to help the French government. Okay, so you come to Paris and stay with me to get the feel of things. I don't object to that. But then you get carried away. It's like the time Bazooka Boy was chasing the Indestructible Iceman."

"What about that?"

"Did you *have* to go live in an igloo at the North Pole for six months?"

"Absolutely!" Woody said, standing up. This time he ignored the water, stepped out of the basin, and sloshed around in his bare feet as he talked. "I had to make sure his new laser-heat-propelling flame really worked!"

"Yeah," Harry said, looking at the ceiling. "You also found out how frostbite works. You're so wrapped up in these characters that sometimes you lose touch with reality. Go home, Woody! Meet a nice girl. Settle down. Relax! Condorman can find enough excitement in New York to last him a lifetime."

"No!" Woody said, rubbing his nose with a tissue. "Superman has the Big Apple all sewn up. Condorman is going international." He sat on the couch next to Harry.

"As for reality and fantasy," he went on,

"look at what you do for a living! What a fantastic life! To be a spy!"

Harry sighed. He really didn't want to go into this again.

"Woody," he said quietly, "I am not a spy."

"Hah!" Woody said, on his feet again and pacing the floor. "Cloak and dagger! CIA! Secret missions! Parachuting behind enemy lines! Memorizing code words! That *has* to be the greatest!"

"I've told you a thousand times, Woody, I am—read my lips, Woody—I am a *file clerk!* No more. No less. Whereas you—"

"Please, Harry. No more lectures."

Harry looked at his watch and sighed again. "Okay, Woody," he said. "No more lectures. I have to go anyway. See you later."

"Harry?"

He stopped on his way to the door. "What?"

"Thanks again," Woody said, smiling. "For saving my life back there. I really appreciate it."

"Forget it. As long as you realize you don't *have* to pull these crazy stunts to make your comic books more believable." He turned toward the door again. "This is real life, Woody. Don't live in a dream world."

"I won't," Woody said. "And Harry?"

Harry turned again, this time to see Woody standing with his arms outstretched.

"Condorman thanks you, too," he said with a grin.

Harry found an unpleasant surprise when he walked into his office. Russ Devlin, his supervisor, was waiting for him.

"Morning, Russ," Harry said. "What's up?"

"You're late," Russ said. "I'm off to the Geneva meeting. I'll be gone for two days, and I want you to keep an eye on things."

"Sure," Harry said, not feeling very sure at all. "But what about the Istanbul papers? We're supposed to make the exchange tomorrow."

"You'll have to take care of that," Russ said, already inching away. "They aren't important anyway."

"But Harrington isn't due back until the weekend," Harry said, his voice shaking just a little.

"We aren't sending Harrington," Russ said. "It's all in the report on your desk. The Russians insist the exchange be handled by civilians."

"Civilians!" Harry said, wide-eyed. "What are they afraid of?"

"They don't want the Chinese to get wind of any of their spies in Turkey."

"Have you recruited the civilian?" Harry asked, near panic.

"That's where you come in," Russ said, stepping into the hall. He walked into an open elevator and pressed a button. "Find someone suitable!" he called through the open doors.

"Me?" Harry yelled as the doors were closing.

Twenty minutes later, Harry was in the computer room waiting for a printout. The computer clerk tore a sheet from the machine and handed it to him.

It didn't take long for Harry to get the sense of the computer's message.

"That's it?" he said to the clerk. The only American tourists going to Turkey are fourteen nuns from Philadelphia?"

"Look again," the clerk said pleasantly, pointing to a line on the printout. "They cancelled and reapplied for Zurich. I think they're a ski club. Sorry I can't help."

The clerk went back to his job and Harry looked again at the printout. Finally, he rolled it into a ball and flung it at a wastebasket. The next moment his face lit up. He went over to a nearby desk, picked up the phone, dialed, and waited.

10

"Woody?" he said, beaming. "Harry here. Listen, buddy, remember how I saved your life this morning?"

Pause.

"Well, how would you like to pay me back?"

Pause.

"I need you to do me a *big* favor."

Pause.

"Well, I'm very happy to hear that, Woody. Say, do you like riding on trains?"

Harry pushed his way through the crowd at the railroad station. He carried a briefcase in one hand and several magazines under the other arm. As he moved along, he swung his head from side to side, looking for Woody.

Suddenly, his head stopped, and so did he— to stare at the sight not ten feet in front of him.

Woody stood before him in a heavy trench coat that had enough flaps on it to qualify as a Condorman outfit. He had the collar pulled up, and he was wearing dark glasses. The brim of his hat was pulled so far down in front that Harry was sure Woody couldn't see a thing. Harry walked up and tapped him on the shoulder.

Woody spun around, his hands inside his coat pockets pointing forward like six-shooters. The hands moved downward when he recognized Harry.

"What's with the getup?" Harry asked.

Woody smiled. "You like it?"

"I hate it." He pulled off Woody's sunglasses and jammed them into his own pocket. "Give me the coat and the hat, Woody."

"Why?" Woody whined. "Come on, Harry!"

"Take them off, Woody! You're a civilian. That's why we picked you. This is definitely *not* a job for Bogart."

He reached up and grabbed Woody's hat. He crumpled it and tried to stuff it inside his jacket pocket.

"Okay, you can have the hat," Woody said, crossing his arms as though he were hugging himself. "But leave me the coat. Please, Harry! It gives me confidence."

"Okay," Harry sighed. "But remember, you're supposed to blend in."

"Got it," Woody said out of the corner of his mouth.

"Give me your wrist," Harry said.

"My wrist?" Woody asked, holding his hands out.

Harry snapped a handcuff around Woody's

right wrist. A chain led from the handcuff to the handle of the briefcase.

"Oooooh!" Woody squealed. "I like that!"

"I figured you would," Harry said. "Here's the key. Don't lose it."

Woody took the key and dropped it into his pants pocket. Harry patted him on the back.

"Thanks, Harry," Woody said seriously. "And don't worry. I won't let the organization down. Even though you've never told me just what the organization is."

"Do me a favor, Woody. When you get on the train, try to get some sleep. Stay out of trouble."

"Hey, you're talking to Woody, remember?"

The conductor announced the last call for the train. Harry and Woody shook hands and Woody walked off. Just before he reached the train, he stopped and turned.

"Harry!" he called. "Where do I get off again?"

"The end of the line, Woody. Istanbul."

"IS—TAN—BUL!" Woody sang. Then he ran to catch the train.

The meeting place in Istanbul was a restaurant. Woody was lucky enough to find a cab driver at the airport who spoke English. He wasn't so sure, however, about his luck when it came time to pay the fare. He handed the driver a combination of dollars, francs, and piasters that might have been a fair rate. On the other hand, it might have been enough to finance the U.S. foreign aid bill for a year.

After the taxi pulled away, Woody stood looking through the small window in the door of the cafe. The place was dark, smoky, and jammed with people. Three musicians were performing on a small stage, but no one seemed to be paying them any mind.

No one paid any attention to Woody either, as he slipped inside and let the door slide shut behind him. His gaze moved slowly across the room as he tried to guess who his contact might be.

Let Harry play down his job all he wants, Woody thought. *This is a James Bond movie, and I'm in it. In fact, I'm the star.*

He tightened his grip on the handle of the briefcase, stuck out his jaw, and moved toward the four steps that led down into the restaurant. Bristling with the confidence that came from wearing his trench coat, he stepped down, and tripped on the top step.

As he pitched forward, he missed, by a fraction of an inch, being stabbed by a flaming sword covered with bits of meat.

The waiter carrying the sword floated by,

not even noticing that he had almost killed an American secret agent on a dangerous mission. When Woody regained his balance, he began struggling through the crowd on his way to a table in the back.

He tripped over someone's foot and this time he fell to the floor. He looked up to see that he was in an alcove furnished with two chairs and a table. A woman was sitting in one of the chairs.

"Excuse me," she said. "I am so sorry."

Woody didn't know much about accents, but hers could pass for Russian. No, it would *be* Russian. After all, this was his movie.

"No, no," he said, getting to his feet. "It was my fault. I should have—"

What stopped him was the sight of the woman. Whoever was helping him cast this movie was certainly on his side. She had skin like satin, eyes like almonds, and her hair fell softly on her shoulders. She was the most beautiful woman Woody had ever seen, in or out of a movie.

"I tripped you with a purpose," she whispered. "I guessed that you were the one I am waiting for."

"Well," Woody whispered back, "that was wonderful. I've never enjoyed falling so much."

16

"I believe we have something to give each other," she said.

"We do?" Woody said dreamily. "Oh, yes, of course. We can give each other wonderful things."

"I speak of documents," she said. "Papers."

"Papers?" Woody asked. "Ooooh, yes, papers. Istanbul, the briefcase. Right."

"The exchange must be discreet," she said, her eyes scanning the room.

Woody sat as close to her as he dared, but not quite as close as he wanted to. His eyes scanned the room, too, as he slipped back into his movie character.

"Of course," he agreed. "An exchange without discreetness is like...it's like...well, it wouldn't be discreet."

She took a package from under the table and put it on the seat between them. It was wrapped in brown paper and tied with heavy cord.

"These are the papers from our side," she said.

"What's your name?" Woody asked.

She stared at him for several seconds, then answered, "Natalia."

"Natalia," he repeated, staring into her eyes.

"Is something wrong?"

"Huh?" Woody asked absently. "No, no. It's just that you're so beautiful—for a spy."

"Spy?" she said, alarmed. "But I . . . you . . . we are both civilians."

"Things," Woody said, leaning forward, "are not always what they seem."

With his chin in his hand and his eyes locked into hers, he leaned forward some more. His elbow slipped off the table, his face kept going, and his chin just missed hitting the edge of the table.

"You're not a civilian?" Natalia asked as Woody straightened up.

He pulled himself to his full sitting height. "In point of fact," he said, "I'm a top-level operative involved in international espionage. I just happened to be passing through. I'm doing a favor for a civilian of my acquaintance."

"Is that so?" Natalia said. Her eyes had stopped scanning the room and had come to rest on a Chinese man who had been watching her. As their eyes met, he got up and slipped into the back room.

Natalia looked at Woody. "Do you have a code name?" she asked.

"Does the name"—Woody paused for effect—"*Condorman* mean anything to you?"

He leaned back for further effect, but there

was no back to the chair. He kept going until his head hit the wall. Then he tried to make it look as though hitting the wall was what he'd had in mind all along.

"Condorman?" Natalia said.

"Yes. Condorman. Vulture of the Western World."

Natalia sat bolt upright. The Chinese man was returning to the room. He was followed closely by three huge companions.

"I must go," she said, grabbing her coat.

"Go?" he said. "Don't be silly. The night is young. We will have dinner together."

"I cannot risk it," she said, edging away from him.

"Please!" Woody said in his real — not his movie—voice. The change seemed to stop her. "Please don't go. I mean, we'll never see each other again. And you're so beautiful."

"Those men," Natalia said, staring at the door. "They are after me."

"We'll leave together," Woody said, not even looking at the door. "They won't try anything if you're with me."

"They will stop at nothing."

"Are you forgetting?" Woody said lightly, getting up and taking her hand. "Condorman. Vulture of the Western World?"

She picked up her package and wrapped her

coat around it. Then she reluctantly let him lead her to the door.

"We are in great danger!" she hissed.

"Danger?" he said loudly. "I laugh at danger. Ha! Double ha!"

When they reached the door, Woody finally saw what he'd been laughing at. He quickly realized that any one of these men could have eaten a tank for breakfast.

"You didn't tell me there were three of them," he said softly to Natalia.

"Step aside," one of the men growled.

"I'm sorry," Woody said politely. "That's impossible."

The man drew out a long, curved knife and held it against Woody's ribs.

"Step aside or die," he rumbled.

Woody turned white, then green. "Well," he said foolishly, "if you feel that strongly about it—"

He threw his hands into the air to show that he meant no harm, and the briefcase, chained to his wrist, came hurtling up and smacked into the chin of the man standing behind him. The man with the knife was so astonished to see his friend fall unconscious that he forgot himself for a second. That was all the time Natalia needed to grab the weapon from his hand.

When Woody realized what she had done, he figured he'd better help. He threw a punch, but the man backed smoothly away from it. Woody's fist went gliding by the man's face, followed closely by the flying briefcase, which hit the thug on the side of the head.

Woody turned to see that the crowd in the restaurant had formed a ring to watch the battle. He also saw the third hood coming at him with a knife.

He backed up and swung the briefcase in a circle over his head. The third attacker stopped to reconsider his position. This gave Woody enough time to spot a waiter, slightly to his left, holding another flaming sword of meat.

Woody stopped swinging the briefcase and his attacker advanced again. Woody reached over, grabbed the flaming sword, and held it in front of him.

The hood had just enough time to dodge the blade, but he wasn't so lucky with the flame. His shirt caught fire and he ran screaming into the street.

Without thinking Woody ran after him. He stopped at the door and muttered, under his breath, "Am I crazy? What am I chasing him for?"

He peered through the little window to

make sure the man was still running, then he turned to look at the other two. They were still unconscious from the blows with the briefcase.

The sound of polite applause made him realize that he had just won a fight. He smiled and bowed to the restaurant patrons. Then he held his hand out. Natalia walked over and took his hand.

In his spy voice Woody said, "I had no idea it would get so messy, Natalia. Sorry I had to get so violent, but it was the only language they understood."

"You are all right?" Natalia asked with a look of such tenderness that Woody got dizzy.

"I'm fine," he said. "And you?"

She smiled. "I was afraid for you."

Grinning, blushing, and straightening his tie—though he wasn't wearing one—Woody said, "Really? That's very nice. But I'll tell you one thing. If I ever come back to Istanbul, this place will be on my 'must miss' list."

They stood smiling at each other for several seconds. Then Natalia unfolded her coat and held the package out to him. He opened the briefcase, took out a package of his own, and exchanged with her.

"Thank you," she said, staring into his eyes. "For everything."

"Oh," Woody said, shuffling his feet, "it was nothing really. I do this sort of thing two, three times a day—"

He stopped talking only because she leaned forward and kissed him. He stared at her as she moved away and opened the door to the street.

"*Au revoir*, Condorman!" she called out. Then she was gone.

Woody stayed in his trance for a few more seconds. Then he snapped out of it. He called her name, rushed through the door, and looked up and down the street.

Natalia was gone. Woody thought for a moment that it had all been a dream. But he knew that wasn't so. He could still smell her perfume. And he could put his hand through the slash in his jacket made by the knife.

_____ *3*

It was a damp, foggy night in Moscow. Natalia was glad to be home at last. A warm bath and a cup of tea were all she wanted before getting into bed.

She unlocked the door to her apartment, went inside, and switched on the light. She pushed the door closed with her foot and let her suitcase fall to the floor. Then she tossed Woody's package on the couch. She heard the man's voice as she was hanging her coat in the closet.

"Good evening, Natalia. Welcome home."

Without turning, she closed her eyes and took a deep breath. "Hello, Sergei," she said. "I wasn't expecting you."

She closed the closet door and turned. Sergei Krokov, second in command in the Soviet secret service, gave her a small bow.

Krokov was a tall, handsome man of about fifty. His clothes, as always, were the latest in Western fashion. His hair was neatly styled and his hands were manicured. He had helped himself to a glass of wine from Natalia's liquor cabinet.

"I'm sure you weren't, my dear," he replied. "Any more than I was expecting you to go to Istanbul."

She walked to the cabinet and poured herself a glass of wine. He watched as she went to the couch and sat down.

"I had to go to Istanbul," she said. "We can't trust the Americans, as I found out."

She sipped her wine, and he sat in a chair across from her.

"Really, my little dove?" he said. "And just what did you find out?"

He reached for her hand, but she pulled away.

"The exchange," she said, "was supposed to be a civilian operation. I distrusted them. And I was right. They sent a top agent."

Krokov tried to hide his surprise at this news, but he wasn't successful. Natalia smiled slightly, pleased at having the upper hand.

"I had the office check him out," she said. "But there was no file on this man. He was good — very smooth, very tough. Perhaps even as good as you, Sergei."

He stood and she looked up at him, taking another sip of her wine. This was even better than she had hoped.

"And his name?" Krokov demanded. "Surely while you were learning how 'tough' and how 'smooth' he was, surely you learned his name."

"He calls himself Condorman."

"Condorman," Krokov said, smirking. "How quaint. Yes, he is good. The way he handled those three Turks was inspiring! If they had got hold of you, who knows what might have happened. It was stupid of you, Natalia, to be seen by a Chinese agent!"

Natalia hadn't seen Krokov this angry in a long time. Her enjoyment began to fade. When she spoke again, it was in the tone of an underling to a superior.

"I felt it was my duty," she said. "We couldn't trust a civilian to have dealt with someone like this Condorman."

Krokov sat down again. "So," he chuckled, "my dear little Natalia — the innocent girl I took from the filing department and trained to be an agent—plans her own operations without informing her benefactor."

She sat up straight and looked at the floor. "That was a long time ago, Sergei," she said. "Things have changed between us."

"Have they?" he said, reaching again for her hand. Once again, she pulled away.

She stood and walked across the room to stare out the window. He walked slowly toward her.

"It's a pity," he said. "Who could have realized you would turn out this way? Requesting more and more assignments in the Western countries. Developing a taste for things you could never buy on an agent's salary. I can't let the Party begin thinking I've gone soft, Natalia."

She turned to face him. "What do you mean?" she asked.

"They are aware of our previous relationship," Krokov said. "They will be watching to see how I deal with the problem of Natalia. That is why I have decided not to take you to Monte Carlo for the meetings with our Arabian friends. You need a little re-education, Natalia."

He was standing in front of her now. She reached out and touched him on the cheek.

"Sergei," she said, "you couldn't be so cruel. You know how much I've been looking forward to Monte Carlo. I know I shouldn't have gone to Istanbul. Forgive me, dear."

She ran her finger along the side of his face and smiled at him. Now it was his turn to pull away.

"No, Natalia. It would be better for all concerned if you remained in Moscow for the time being." He turned away and put his wine glass on the table.

"You monster!" she screamed. "I wish you were dead!"

"Temper, temper," he said laughing. "It's a good thing I'm still fond of you, Natalia. If anyone else spoke to me that way—"

"Go ahead!" she yelled. "What can you do with me? Kill me? Send me to prison? I hate you!"

She fell onto the couch, sobbing. Krokov reached down and took her hand. He gave it a light kiss, picked up his hat, and turned toward the door. He stopped before he opened it and listened to her sobs.

"Good night, my dear Natalia," he said. "And dry your eyes. You know I can't stand to see a beautiful woman cry—even when it is only an act."

After he had let himself out, she took off her

shoe and flung it at the closed door. Then she began crying again, but now it was for real.

She opened her purse and pulled out a handkerchief. A book of matches fell to the floor, and she reached down and picked them up.

They were from the Istanbul cafe. As she stared at them, she could see Woody's face and she smiled, even while she was crying.

Harry had fallen asleep on the couch. His snoring didn't bother Woody, who was deeply involved in his latest creation. He'd been working all day and night, and the floor was littered with discarded sketches.

Now he was finished. He leaned back and beamed at his work. It was a new character for his comics. It was beautiful, it was exciting, and he loved it.

"Harry!" he called. "Isn't she beautiful?"

He held his work up for Harry to admire. Harry grunted and turned over, without opening his eyes.

Woody held the drawing at arm's length. "My Laser Lady," he said softly.

Laser Lady, in tights and a cape, her name emblazoned across the top of the poster, gazed back at him. She looked a great deal like Natalia.

"My Laser Lady," Woody repeated.

First thing in the morning Harry knocked on Russ Devlin's office door. "Harry?" Russ called from inside.

"Yeah."

The door opened and Harry moved to go inside.

"Not here," Russ said. "Meet me in front of the building in five minutes." Then he closed the door.

Harry walked to the elevator and pressed the down button. The doors opened, he stepped inside, and he heard the doors close behind him.

What is this all about? he wondered. He had

delivered Woody's package. The mission seemed to have gone right. What did Russ want with him? And why did it have to be in front of the building?

He stepped out at the ground floor and walked toward the exit. Another elevator arrived and Russ stepped out.

"Russ," Harry said. "What's going on?"

Russ put his finger to his lips. He took Harry's arm and steered him to the door. Once outside, he looked up and down the street.

"I had to be sure we wouldn't be overheard," Russ explained as they walked slowly down the street.

"What's up?" Harry asked.

"Tell me about Condorman," Russ said.

"Condorman?!"

"Condorman," Russ repeated.

"Condorman," Harry began, "is...well, he's what you call a superhero. In a comic book."

Russ raised his eyebrows. "A comic book?"

"Yeah," Harry said. "You know, like Donald Duck, Popeye, Superman?"

"He isn't a real person?"

"Who?" Harry asked, not understanding why they were having this conversation.

"Condorman!" Russ said with annoyance.

"Uh, no, Russ. Comic book characters aren't real people. Donald Duck, for example, isn't a real duck. He's just a drawing."

Was he really saying these things to his boss?

"Interesting," Russ said, as though he hadn't really heard what Harry was saying.

Harry was determined to keep up his end of the conversation. "I don't know how interesting it is," he said. "I mean, every kid knows that. I've known it all my life. Uh, Russ, haven't you ever read a comic book?"

"Harry," Russ said, "Condorman is a real person."

Maybe the job was getting to be too much for Russ. Harry had heard of other guys cracking under the strain. Probably the best thing to do would be to humor him."

"Oh, if you say so, Russ," he said brightly. "*I* thought he was a cartoon figure. Uh, is that all you wanted to talk about?"

Russ stopped walking. Harry stopped and faced him.

"Listen carefully, Harry," Russ said. "We have a Russian agent who wants to defect. This Russian insists that we use one particular agent to handle the defection. Apparently they've worked together or something. We were given the code name of the agent, but we have no record of it. Harry, it's vital that we find this man and use him to handle this operation. I want you to check every file we have. Find out who is using the code name Condorman!"

Harry's mouth hung open. His eyes glazed over and he stared at his boss.

"Is something wrong?" Russ asked.

"No," Harry said weakly. "I know who uses that name."

Two hours later, Woody sat at his drawing table, staring in disbelief at his friend.

"Harry," he said, "are you serious?"

"Very," Harry said, falling onto the couch.

"I could get killed!" Woody said.

Harry jumped up and walked to the drawing table. "Woody, it isn't dangerous. Just a simple defection."

"Simple defection! Simple for you, maybe. I delivered some simple papers in Istanbul and nearly got shish-kebabbed by three Turkish rhinos!"

"You'll have every protection," Russ said, coming in from the kitchen with a bottle of beer. "The Bear is very important to us."

"Bear?" Woody asked. "What bear?"

"Uh, Woody," Harry said, getting between him and Russ, "in the spy game we're quite fond of using code names. Sort of keeps things interesting. The Bear is the Russian who wants to defect."

Woody got up and walked to the other side of the room. He wanted as much space as possible between himself and these two members of the spy game.

"Sorry, fellas," he said. "I refuse to place my fragile life on the line for anyone who goes under the code name of The Bear. The Pussycat maybe. But I'll pass on The Bear."

"It would be an act of patriotism," Russ said between sips of his beer.

"Forget patriotism!" Woody snapped. "I have my family to think of!"

"What family?" Harry asked.

"Gopher Boy!" Woody yelled. "And Sponge Man. There are also deadlines to think of. Condorman and Laser Lady make their debut as a team next week."

"Do you realize," Russ asked, "that we are talking about one of the most important defections of this decade?"

"But I'm no spy!" Woody whined.

"Come on, Woody," Harry kidded. "A little cloak, a little dagger. You'll love it."

"No, no, no," Woody said firmly. "Look, I'd like to help. But I don't know anything about shooting or blowing up bridges."

Russ glared at Harry. "Do something," he muttered under his breath.

"Woody!" Harry said. "What do you mean you don't know anything? What about Gopher Boy and the Groundhog People? How about Sponge Man in the Sahara?"

"They're comic books, Harry!"

"Yeah," Harry said, getting really excited. "But everything in them works!"

"Well—" Woody said, uncertainly.

"Russ," Harry said, "this guy is nuts. He won't put anything in his comics unless it's tested and proven. Look at these."

Harry picked up a stack of Woody's drawings. He spread them out on the couch for Russ to look at.

"Take a look," Harry urged. "Cars that do everything but make their own gas. Planes that would knock your eyes out.

"But—" Woody began.

"But what?" Harry interrupted. "Here's your chance, Woody! Out of the inkwell, and into real life. And your Uncle Sam will foot the bill!"

Woody's eyes widened. "You mean," he

said, "if Condorman accepts this assignment, he could—I mean, I could do it my own way? Use my own equipment?"

"The chance of a lifetime, Woody!" Harry said. "Whatever you have in mind for Condorman next, the organization will build it for you at Uncle Sam's expense. Right, Russ?

"I don't know whether—" Russ said.

"*Right*, Russ?" Harry insisted.

"Right," Russ said. He had no idea where this simple word might lead him. But he needed Woody's help desperately.

"I don't know," Woody said, turning and staring out the window. "It's tempting...but, no." He turned back to face them. "I'm sorry, guys. I'll have to say no."

Harry fell back onto the couch in defeat. Russ sighed. Then he found himself staring at the drawing of Laser Lady hanging on the wall.

His face lit up. He took some photos from his pocket, looked at them, looked back at the poster, and smiled. Then he turned to Woody.

"Believe me, Mr. Wilkins," Russ said, "we wouldn't ask you to do this if it weren't for one fact."

"What's that?" Woody asked suspiciously.

"The Bear," Russ said, "insisted that *you* be the escort."

36

Even more suspiciously, Woody asked, "How would The Bear know anything about me?"

Russ held the photographs out in front of him and smiled broadly. "You've already met her," he said. "In Istanbul. Natalia Rambova of the KGB."

Woody took the photos, looked at them, and practically melted before their very eyes. Harry stared at him, dumbfounded.

Woody and Harry arrived at Russ's office early the next morning. They sat silently waiting for him.

Harry was silent because he was no longer sure of his position in this affair. He'd started as the "spy" who recruited a civilian to carry out a mission. Now the civilian was dealing directly with the boss, on the verge of carrying out something infinitely more exciting than anything Harry had ever done in the service.

Woody was silent because he was thinking of Natalia. He'd been up all night working on the sketches that now lay on Russ's desk. He'd worked like a madman, driven by the thought that he would see Natalia again after all.

Russ came in, tossed his coat over a chair, and went straight to his desk. The sketch for the cover read CONDORMAN AND THE ESCAPE OF THE BEAR. The art showed Woody — as Condorman — leading a bear across a map of Europe. Russ went through the other sketches quickly, pausing to study the machinery and gadgets Woody had designed.

He turned the last one over, looked up, and said, "Impossible. Totally out of the question."

Only a little taken aback, Woody spoke quietly but firmly. "You said you would do this my way. With my designs."

"Yes," Russ said, sitting at his desk, "but this will cost us a fortune. This is a tricky transfer, I know. But couldn't you simplify it a bit?"

Harry jumped in, mostly to remind them that he was still a part of this deal. "Woody, Russ has a point. He wants you to bring him The Bear, not a comic book."

"If I don't get this equipment," Woody said, "then I don't get The Bear."

Harry looked from Woody to Russ. "Your move, Russ," he said.

"I don't know," Russ said, looking again at the sketches and shaking his head.

"Of course," Harry offered, "if all else fails, we can always go to Plan B."

After only a short pause Russ looked up. "Okay," he said. "Get Fabrication started on making this stuff immediately."

Woody smiled. He stood up to shake hands with Russ, but Harry hustled him out of the office before the decision could be changed. They hurried down the hall to Fabrication.

"Harry," Woody said, "what's Plan B?"

"I don't know," Harry said. "But I should have something ready by the time you get to Yugoslavia."

The ancient castle stood on a hill somewhere in the Yugoslav countryside. Dawn was just beginning to break, as an old man slowly made his way up the hill toward the castle.

He was a gypsy, dressed in a colorful collection of rags and castoff clothes. He used a crooked walking stick to support himself on his way up the hill.

He walked through the rusty gate of the deserted castle and looked up at the building. Every tower, every terrace, every gargoyle threw a shadow that could be hiding an attacker.

The gypsy took something from his shirt and looked at it. It was a comic book with a drawing of a castle that looked very much like the one in front of him.

Woody smiled at his artwork and slipped it back inside his shirt. Just as he checked his watch, he heard a soft whistle from behind him.

He turned and saw someone step from the shadows. It was another figure dressed in a gypsy outfit. Woody couldn't keep himself from trembling.

"Natalia?" he said. "Is it you?"

"Yes," she answered, walking up to him. "I knew you would come."

Woody let go of the breath he'd been holding. He and Natalia stared at each other for some seconds. Then he grinned.

"Hi!" he said. "I hope you don't mind the gypsy disguise. I figured you'd look good in anything."

She smiled and he took her hand. Then he leaned forward to kiss her.

"We should hurry," she whispered. "We could still be discovered."

"You're right," he said, backing away. "Come on."

While a dog howled in the distance, Woody led Natalia out through the gate. He used the walking stick to keep his balance as they rushed down the hill.

"Everything's prepared," he whispered. "We should be able to leave the country without a problem."

Before she had a chance to say anything, two men stepped out from the side of the path. They pointed guns at Woody and Natalia.

"Halt!" one of them ordered. "An escape at dawn. Very romantic, Comrade. And who is your American friend here?"

Woody stepped between Natalia and the Russian agent. He held out his right hand and smiled.

"We haven't met," he said. "I'm Condorman. Vulture of the Western World. Daring young man and all-around good egg."

The second agent slapped his hand out of the way. "Keep back!" he growled.

"You guys don't understand," Woody said. "I'm really a double agent. I'm on your side. I'm delivering some secret information to The Bear here. We're old comrades—from Istanbul."

The first agent glared at Natalia. "Is that your story, too?" he asked.

"Yes," Natalia said. "It is the truth."

"Really?" the agent said, sneering. "Krokov will be most interested. He has suspected your defection for some time. We have been following you for weeks."

"Hand over your weapons," the second agent said.

Natalia slowly reached inside her coat. She withdrew a small silver pistol and held it out. The second agent grabbed it from her.

Woody slowly backed away from the two men. "I don't have one," he said. "Condorman doesn't carry a gun. It's against my code."

"What are you talking about?" the first agent demanded.

"Guns scare me," Woody said, smiling and taking another step back. "The noise mostly. All I carry is my trusty old cane here."

He held the cane up to show them. As they looked at it he pressed the handle. All he heard was a click. Astounded, he stared at the cane.

"They didn't load it?" he screamed, and slammed the tip of the cane on the ground in anger. Suddenly the silence was broken by machine-gun fire tearing out of the end of the cane.

The recoil sent Woody hurtling backwards in a circle. He had no control over the machine-gun cane. Natalia and the two agents covered their heads and fell to the ground. One of the agents hit his head on a rock and passed out.

Bullets ricocheted off rocks and trees as Woody danced in response to the gun. When he finally ran out of ammunition, he fell, sitting on the ground next to Natalia. She looked up at him from her crouched position.

"Hair trigger," Woody said with a nervous smile. "Fastest cane in the West."

"Look out!" Natalia screamed.

Woody fell back and rolled over to see what had scared her. The second agent was leaping for him, but Woody never saw him. As Woody rolled over, his feet happened to be in the air, the agent happened to get them right in the stomach, and Woody happened to find the cane next to his hand.

He grabbed it and jumped up. The agent lay stunned on the ground. Woody walked over and smacked him on the head with the cane. The agent fell over, unconscious.

Woody looked at the cane, then at Natalia. "Multi-purpose," he said. "Let's go!"

He grabbed her hand, pulled her from the ground, and led her down the road. They soon came to an old, beat-up truck in a small clearing. The back was covered with canvas. It looked like a gypsy caravan with a motor.

Natalia jumped into the front of the truck. Woody stood outside the driver's side, fumbling through his pockets.

"Hurry!" she said. "What are you doing?"

"I'm trying to find the keys!" he said. "This always happens to me. I should have tied them around my neck — ah, here they are!"

He hopped in and started the truck. It lumbered slowly onto the road, and just as slowly moved away from the castle.

Natalia watched the road through her window to see if they were being followed. There was nothing behind them. She pulled her head back in and sat back.

"You are not nervous?" she asked.

"Me? Condorman? Nervous?" Woody decided it would be better not to answer such a question directly.

They bounced along in nervous silence for a while. Then he said, "So — you decided to defect, huh?"

Natalia nodded. "Things have not been easy for me at home. I have been thinking of it for some time."

"Why didn't you do it from Istanbul?"

"I wasn't sure then," Natalia answered. "I made my decision after I got back. It was because of what happened between Krokov and me."

"Krokov?" Woody asked.

"The man those agents talked about. He was my teacher, and also—"

He waited. Then he understood what she wasn't going to say.

"Oh," he said. "I see. Well, go on."

"I would prefer not to talk about it now. The memories are too painful."

"This Krokov," Woody said. "You aren't married to him, by any chance?"

"No," she said, smiling at him. "I am a single woman."

Woody smiled back. "I'm glad to hear that. Maybe I can show you the sights when we get to Paris."

"That would be wonderful," Natalia said. "I would love to again visit the Hotel LeClair and the Club Jazz. I miss them so."

"Uh," Woody said, deflated, "I never heard of those."

"Well, then," Natalia said, "I will show *you* the Paris that *I* know."

"Terrific," Woody mumbled. "You're the one who's defecting from Russia, and you're going to show me the Western world."

She smiled at him again. They rode in silence for a mile or so. Then Natalia let out a long, sad sigh.

"What's wrong?" Woody asked.

"I was thinking," she said, "I'll never see my village again. It makes me sad. America is so far away."

Woody brightened at this chance to take control again. "But you'll love it when you get there," he said. "New York—those buildings! And the Grand Canyon, and autumn in New England! Thanksgiving, baseball, the senior prom! Hey, have you ever eaten a Big Mac?"

"Big Mac?" she laughed. "What is that?"

"What is it?" he said, astounded. "It's a...well, you put some...and you cover it with...oh, you'll love it when you taste it! I promise!"

She leaned toward him. "You are so sweet," she said. "Now I am happy again." When she kissed him on the cheek, the truck swerved into the bushes. Woody steered it out of the bushes, and they bounced down the road, laughing.

Krokov stood looking out at the water from
the terrace of an elaborate Monte Carlo estate.
Twenty feet below him, six growling guard
dogs and four agents kept watch on the gate.

He was here for a series of high-level meetings with a group of Arab sheiks. For the
moment, however, his attention was directed
at another problem.

He was listening on the telephone. What he
was hearing made the veins on his neck stand
out.

"But how is that possible?" he roared into

the phone. "I had two men following her! No! I want her alive! Death would be too good for the little traitor!"

He paused and listened again. When he spoke again his tone was more controlled.

"The man is expendable. I don't care what happens to him. Send out the Brochnoviatch. And see to it that Morovich is personally in charge. That's right... Morovich."

Krokov slammed the receiver into the cradle. The sound that came from his throat was not very different from the snarling of the dogs below.

It was mid-morning in the tiny village on the Yugoslav seacoast. Under the warm sun, shopkeepers greeted housewives as they did their day's marketing. Several old men sat talking quietly in the village square and nearby, a group of children were playing soccer in a narrow street. The sound of flute music drifted from one of the apartments above the butcher shop.

One of the old men paused in what he was saying. He thought he heard a faint buzz, as though a swarm of bees had begun to circle overhead.

The flute music stopped and the buzz became louder. A shopkeeper looked up, expecting to see airplanes. Two housewives did the same.

The sound changed from a buzz to a low roar. The children stopped playing. They looked alarmed. Mothers hurried out to find their children and rush them inside.

The old men got up and scurried indoors. Shopkeepers began locking up their doors. The roar had become frighteningly loud. Everyone in town knew what it was.

The Brochnoviatch was coming to their village!

In no time at all the entire square was deserted. Doors had been locked and shades drawn. The roar was ear-splitting now. The Brochnoviatch came tearing into the village square.

Five fierce, pantherlike racing cars slowed and came to a snarling halt in the square. Each was painted a deep black. Their windows were two-way mirrors, so that anyone looking into the car would see only his own reflection. Without a visible driver, each car seemed to be self-propelled, to have a mind of its own.

But that was only an illusion. There were drivers in these death machines. And no matter how fierce the cars looked, they were nothing compared to the minds that operated them.

The Brochnoviatch was a Russian task force that was called out for only the most serious of missions. These drivers were among the best-trained killers in the world. They would let nothing stand between them and the successful completion of their mission.

The villagers trembled inside their homes and stores. What could these monsters want with their quiet little town?

Four of the cars sat in the square, their engines idling. The fifth moved back and forth, as though studying the town's layout. It was like the other four, except in one respect. It had a small radar unit on its roof.

Morovich, the leader of the Brochnoviatch, drove this car from one end of the square to the other. He was, indeed, studying the streets.

Like the other drivers, he was dressed in a black racing suit, black gloves, and a black helmet. Beneath his visor was a small microphone through which he could direct the others.

He stopped his car and raised his visor. He put his hand to his right eye and squeezed. Out popped the steel ball he used in place of a glass eye.

Morovich rubbed the ball between his fingers. It was something he always did for luck before a mission. He put the steel ball back into its socket and grinned.

Then he slapped the visor down, held the microphone close to his lips, and barked out an order.

The other cars immediately took off, each in a different direction. Each ended up on a different narrow side street just off the square. When his men were in place, Morovich took his position on a fifth side street.

The menacing engines were turned off. The village was silent, but only for less than a minute. The silence was broken by the puttering sound of a gypsy truck heading into town.

As they neared the square, Woody said, "It's like a storybook town. Look at it. And it's so quiet."

Natalia's eyes darted from one side of the street to the other. "It's too quiet," she said.

"What do you mean?" Woody asked.

"The people," Natalia said, worried. "Where are the people?"

As they drove through the empty square, Woody said, "Natalia, you have to learn to calm down. Relax. Relaxing is a very American thing to do."

"Something is wrong," she said.

They reached the end of the village and drove out. The chugging of the truck was still the only sound to be heard.

"Something is wrong," Natalia repeated.

"There's nothing to worry about," Woody said, smiling. "We're home free."

Back in the village five engines fired up simultaneously. Five black cars moved back into the square and slid into a V-formation, with Morovich at the head. The formation took off after the truck.

Bouncing along a mile or two out of the village, Woody kept up his patter. "Just take deep breaths," he said. "Sit back and enjoy the scenery."

"Krokov would do anything to get me back," Natalia said.

"Forget Krokov," Woody said. "You're with me now."

She leaned her head back and closed her eyes. Woody glanced in his side-view mirror, then did a double take to make sure he wasn't imagining something.

"Uh, Natalia," Woody said uncertainly.

"What is it?" she asked without opening her eyes.

"You tell me," he said.

She opened her eyes and looked at him. He pointed to the back. She stuck her head out the window and looked at the road behind them.

With her head still out the window, she screamed, "The Brochnoviatch!"

"The Brock—what?" Woody said, keeping his eyes on the road.

The cars were dangerously close as Natalia pulled her head back in. She looked at Woody pleadingly.

"We can't outrun them in this old truck!" she said.

"You have a point there," Woody said, only slightly less calm than usual. "But—"

Natalia watched as he pressed a button near the steering wheel. She felt herself sinking, as though her seat had been turned into a slide.

They both slid down into what seemed like the floor of the truck. Natalia was astounded to find herself sitting next to Woody in front of a complicated control panel.

A new steering wheel appeared in front of Woody. The center of the control panel contained a TV screen. The rest was a mass of levers and buttons.

Woody pressed one of these buttons, and a split picture showed up on the screen. One half showed what was obviously the road ahead of them. The other half showed the five black cars chasing them.

Woody's hand moved to another button. Natalia watched the screen and saw pieces of the truck bouncing along the road behind them. The panther cars stopped and pulled off the road.

The debris took up enough road space to give Woody a running start. The machine he was driving, built and equipped by Harry's department, would have made the Batmobile look like a Model T.

It was painted in six different flaming colors, dominated by yellow — the color of Condorman's suit. It was low and sleek, painted with huge feathers.

It was also covered with hinges. Natalia was in for several more surprises.

"This is fantastic!" she cried.

"Yeah," Woody laughed. "But like the man said, 'You ain't seen nothing yet.'"

The pursuers were back on the road now, once again in their V-formation. At nearly two hundred miles an hour, they were soon on Woody's tail.

Natalia stared at the video screen. Yelling over the roar of engine, she said, "They're right behind us! What do we do now?"

"We press another button," Woody said.

That button caused a panel to rise up across

the back of his car. Each side of it held a rocket launcher.

A corner of the video screen carried the message, READY TO FIRE. Woody pressed a third button, and two rockets tore in the direction of the Brochnoviatch.

The drivers were already breaking their formation. They glided to the sides of the road, and the rockets went screaming between them.

"I don't believe it!" Woody cried. "I missed!"

Another button brought an extension arm out on each side of the car. Once again the screen read, READY TO FIRE.

Woody fired, and the five cars formed a single file in the center of the road. The rockets shot harmlessly past them.

The screen read, ALL ROCKETS FIRED. For the first time, Woody began to look worried. He shot past an intersection. Seconds later, he watched the screen as two of the cars peeled off into the intersection in opposite directions. The other three stayed close behind.

"Who are those guys?" Woody demanded.

"The Brochnoviatch," Natalia answered. "They're the KGB Pursuit Squadron. Superb drivers."

"I'll say!"

"And each one a dedicated killer."

"Killers!" he said. "Then I'd better try something else!"

He pressed yet another button. Two more projections arose. These were in front of the car, angled so that they pointed to the sky. Woody fired, the rockets took off, and they rose into the air. They quickly ran out of fuel, and a small parachute opened on each one.

The two rockets drifted back to earth. Woody watched them carefully through the slit in his windshield.

"This has to work," he said. "I saw it in a Roadrunner cartoon."

A digital readout on the panel told him where the rockets were and where the three targets were. He watched and waited. Suddenly, he leaned forward and pressed a button.

The rockets came plummeting to the ground. They fell in front of one of the black cars and blew it off the road.

"One down!" Woody said.

The screen showed the other two getting closer than ever. He pulled a switch and a burst of flame shot out of his exhaust.

The two cars slowed to avoid the flame. But

they kept up with Woody, staying just out of the flame's reach.

Suddenly, the real threat was from the front. Racing toward them was one of the cars that had turned off at the intersection. The road was too narrow for either of them to turn off.

"Stop!" Natalia screamed. "He's crazy! He'll kill us all!"

"Nothing doing," Woody said. "That's just what he wants us to do."

He hit another button. A steel ramp snapped out of the hood. A smaller ramp slid down from the roof and covered the windshield.

The two cars came head-on at each other, two other black cars right behind Woody.

"Close your eyes and pray," Woody said. "I swear it worked on paper."

The black car hit Woody's ramp at full speed. It went up the ramp and flew over his car. It came crashing down on the two cars behind him. All three black cars went up in a burst of flame. Woody cheered.

"There is one more," Natalia said. "There were five when we first saw them."

"Who's counting?" Woody said, laughing. "I have a feeling we've seen the last of them."

58

But Morovich had been watching the last few minutes from a nearby mountain. He now took a shortcut and waited for Woody on a side road.

When Woody shot by, Morovich took off after him. He pulled up even with Woody on Natalia's side and lowered his window. His steel eye reflected the sunlight, and his smile seemed to drip blood.

"Morovich!" Natalia gasped as his window slid back up.

"You know that guy?" Woody asked, pulling away.

"He's a homicidal maniac!" Natalia sobbed.

"You hang around with some strange people," Woody said. "Don't you know any nice accountants?"

"Why do you joke all the time?" she yelled between sobs. "This is not a game!"

"I know that," Woody said seriously. "That's why I joke."

Morovich began bumping Woody's car from behind. Even with the roar of the two engines, Natalia was sure she could hear his insane laughter as he tried to force them off the road.

"You've got to stop him!" she screamed.

"I know that!" Woody said. "The question is, *how?*"

"Push something!"

"I'm all pushed out!"

They raced through a small village and Morovich had to slam on his brakes to avoid running into a truck. This gave Woody a small lead. When he spotted the pier up ahead, he aimed straight for it and accelerated. Morovich was back in position, slowly closing the distance between them.

"Woody!" Natalia screeched. "There's nothing but the sea ahead of us!"

Still Woody accelerated. He was almost smiling now.

"We're going to die!" Natalia moaned.

"We're not going to die," Woody said calmly. "We're in big trouble. But we're *not* going to die."

Pedestrians scampered out of the way of the two roaring cars. Woody kept his eyes on the pier ahead of him. Morovich was right behind them.

Terrified, Natalia screamed, "What are you doing? We'll drown!"

Woody reached for a button. The pier ended, and the car sailed out over the water. Morovich came to a screeching halt just as his front wheels reached the end of the planks.

Woody pressed his last button, and two extensions unfolded from the sides of the car. What splashed down into the water was not a car, but a hydrofoil.

It bobbed along the surface of the water. Woody grinned and gunned the engine. The boat motored away from the pier, and Morovich threw his helmet to the ground and stamped on it.

"Escaped again!" Krokov sputtered. "And in a gypsy truck!"

Morovich had driven straight to Monte Carlo the minute Woody's hydrofoil had disappeared from sight. Now he stood before his superior, cradling his smashed helmet under his arm.

"The gypsy truck," he said apologetically, "turned into a race car."

"But *you* had the Brochnoviatch!"

"Yes, but—" Morovich hesitated. He hated having to repeat these details. "But the race car turned into a boat. Right before my very eye."

"You idiot!" Krokov screamed, slamming

his open hand on the desk in front of him. He picked up a folder from the desk and waved it in front of Morovich.

"Have you seen this report on this man, this *Condorman*? This Wilkins is an amateur! *Do you understand?* He is not an agent of the *CIA! He is a comic book writer!* We shall be a laughingstock at home!"

He paused and glared at Morovich, who stared at the floor, saying nothing.

"Get out of my sight!" Krokov roared. "Before I pluck out your other eye!"

"Please, Comrade," Morovich said. "I ask only one thing. One more chance to get at this Condorman."

Krokov stared back. What choice did he have? Morovich was his most reliable — and most vicious—agent. Now, in addition to his general sadistic tendencies, he had a personal reason for wanting to succeed at this mission.

Krokov lit a cigarette and picked up a pointer from his desk. He walked over to a wall map and stared at it. Then he turned to Morovich.

"Very well," he said. "You shall have your chance, my dear Morovich." He aimed the tip of the pointer at a spot on the map. "They have to land somewhere on the northern coast of Italy, if my calculations are correct."

"I am sure that they are, Comrade Commissar."

"And this time," Krokov said, spinning to face Morovich again, "there will be no escape. Because this time, I have a plan."

Keeping his eyes on Morovich, he walked to his desk and pressed the intercom button.

"Vito," he said.

"Yes, Comrade Commissar," said a voice through the intercom.

"Contact Barrazini. We are going to collect on an old debt. Tell him what I want him to do."

The deserted hydrofoil sat on a beach in northwestern Italy. No one had seen the two people climb out of it and run toward the nearby woods. They were already an hour away from the beach when a policeman rode his bike up to the boat.

He took a piece of paper out of his inside jacket pocket and read the description of the getaway boat. He looked again at the vehicle in front of him. Then he smiled, hopped on his bike, and rode off to call in his discovery.

Not many miles from the beach, Woody and Natalia were trudging along a dirt road. They did what they could to stay hidden among the trees, but every now and then they had to face a clearing.

"Where are we?" Natalia asked wearily.

"I don't know," Woody said, walking a few steps in front of her. "But don't worry. We're safe now."

"How can you say that?" she asked in astonishment. She sat on the side of the road and he came back to sit next to her.

"Logic," he said. "We don't know where we are. So it stands to reason Krokov doesn't know either."

"You don't know Krokov," Natalia said sadly. "Perhaps we should not have abandoned the car."

"We had to," Woody said, helping her up and leading her again along the road. "It was a one-way conversion. Once it turned into a boat, that was it. I admit I goofed on that design."

Hardly hearing him, Natalia looked off into the distance. Her face lit up, and she pointed.

"Look!" she cried. "Over there!"

It was an old barn, less than half a mile from the road. Further on they could see a small house, but it was far enough away so they could head straight for the barn without being seen.

"Maybe we can spend the night there,"

Woody said, pulling Natalia after him. "Tomorrow we'll find a phone. I'll call Harry, and we'll be home in no time."

Inside the barn they found a few chickens, two cows, and a hayloft overhead. They climbed up to the loft.

While Natalia made a bed of straw, Woody looked out the window openings. He could see for miles in every direction and the only living creatures were cows and horses. There wasn't a human being in sight.

He turned to see Natalia testing the bed she'd just made.

"Oh, it's perfect," she said. "There's just enough room for the two of us."

Woody swallowed hard and thought about Morovich and Krokov. "You sleep," he said nervously. "I'll keep guard."

Natalia sat up with a look of surprise. "Are you afraid of me?" she asked softly.

"No, no, it isn't that," Woody said. "It's old one-eye. What if he finds us?"

"But you have to sleep," she said. She reached up, took his hand, and gently pulled him onto the hay.

"Sleep?" he said, his head falling on the hay against his will. "For Condorman, sleep is a luxury. I can go without it for days...."

She slid her hand from his forehead over his eyes. They were closed before he finished his last sentence. He was already asleep when she bent over to kiss him on the cheek.

Three hours later, they were in a jail cell. The local police had fanned out from the hydrofoil and had found the two sleeping escapees with little trouble.

Before either of them was fully awake, they had been hustled into separate police cars and driven to the jail.

Woody had protested all the way there, but he'd gotten no response. He wasn't even sure the policemen knew what he was saying.

Natalia walked into the cell and sat on the bunk. As the bars clanged shut, Woody directed his complaints to the retreating guard's back.

"Hey, you!" he yelled. "There's been a mistake! We haven't done anything wrong. You have the wrong couple!"

The guard returned with a rolled-up newspaper. He tossed it between the bars and walked away again.

Woody picked up the paper and unrolled it. There on the front page were separate photos of him and Natalia.

He couldn't read Italian. But he'd seen enough sensational news stories to know they were in trouble.

Natalia took the paper and looked it over. "It says we killed a man in Monte Carlo," she said calmly.

"We haven't even been in Monte Carlo!" Woody protested.

"Krokov is behind this," she told him.

"Guard!" Woody called, grabbing the bars with both hands. "This is all a mistake, I tell you!"

For some reason, the guard decided to answer him this time — and in English.

"You won't be here long, you murdering pigs!" he said, spitting toward their cell. "The authorities from Monte Carlo are on their way."

"Krokov's men!" Natalia gasped.

The guard walked away and Natalia slumped on the cot again. Woody stared into space.

"Oh, Gopher Boy, what would you do now?" he said, half-aloud.

While Woody thought about Gopher Boy and Natalia thought about being tortured, the door at the end of the corridor opened. A little man came in and handed a card to the guard.

The man had a mustache and he wore a long

coat and a hat pulled down over his eyes. *Such an obvious disguise*, Woody thought.

The guard handed back the man's identification, and then led him down the corridor. As they approached the cell, the bearded man reached into his coat and took out two sets of handcuffs.

"The inspector is here from Monte Carlo," the guard said, unlocking the cell.

"You mean from Krokov," Woody said. Then he turned to the little man. "You think this is it, fella? You think we're licked? We know who sent you. And remember, I am an American citizen!"

The man paid him no attention. He took Woody's right wrist and slapped a handcuff around it. Natalia's left wrist was locked into the other half.

He put another cuff around Woody's left wrist and put his own right wrist in the other half. The guard stood off to the side, admiring the security precautions they used in Monte Carlo.

The little man began to lead his two prisoners down the corridor. Woody resisted, because he couldn't think of any reason to cooperate.

"You won't answer me, huh?" he taunted. "Do you even speak English? What language *do* they speak in Monte Carlo anyway?"

They were now about ten feet from the guard. The little man reached up and grabbed Woody's shirt collar, pulling his head down.

"Hey, Ugly American," he whispered. "Remember Plan B? This is it! Now shut up!"

Woody gazed past the mustache and the hat. Inside that little old man was Harry. Big, young, wonderful Harry!

Several policemen watched as the handcuffed trio climbed into the front seat of Harry's car. Harry waved to the policemen and started up the motor.

"I told you we'd get out of this, Natalia," Woody whispered. "He's not from Krokov. He's Harry. Harry's one of us."

"I prefer to think of *you*," Harry said, "as one of *us*. But only for the time being."

The car inched out to the road. Harry didn't want to look too anxious to get away from the police station. Once on the road he began to pick up speed.

"Give me the key, Harry," Woody said.

"Later," Harry said. "Let's make sure we're away from the police first. Besides, the Russians aren't far behind. You're all over the front page."

"Does Russ know about this?" Woody asked.

"Yeah. He's working on the rest of the plan. 'Bazooka Boy Meets Hannibal Smith,' wasn't it?"

"Right!" Woody said, grinning. "One of my favorites!"

Just outside the village, they saw a car stop in the road up ahead. The driver had stepped out of the car to talk to a passing sheepherder. Three other men sat inside.

Harry slowed down and stopped. The driver turned to look at them.

"Morovich!" said Woody and Natalia at the same time.

Harry did a quick U-turn. Morovich hopped into his car and did the same.

"The keys, Harry!" Woody yelled. Locked between Harry and Natalia, he couldn't even turn to see how close Morovich was.

Harry fumbled in his jacket pocket with his left hand. He tried to get into his right pocket, but he was chained to Woody on that side. The car swerved crazily.

Natalia reached over Woody and into Harry's right jacket pocket. She withdrew the keys and unlocked herself from Woody.

Woody then separated himself from Harry, who could now drive with two free hands. The car still swerved, but now it was because Harry considered this a good evasive action.

He turned down a tiny alley. Morovich was going too fast to follow him. He shot past the alley, slammed on his brakes, and backed up.

The alley turned out to be a dead end. Harry stopped the car and three of them jumped out and ran as Morovich's car tore into the alley. But there was nowhere for it to go. Four Russians jumped out and ran after their prey.

Harry came out of the alley first. "Over there!" he said, pointing across a wide street.

"A church!" Woody panted, following Harry across the street. "Terrific. It's time for some prayers."

The three of them raced up to the door. It was open and they could see a wedding ceremony going on at the altar. They stopped to compose themselves, then they quietly walked inside and sat among the friends and family.

Seconds later Morovich and his henchmen entered the church. They looked around, spotted the three fugitives, and headed toward them.

The priest was beginning the ceremony. "We are gathered here to join Pietro Pavolini and Gina Gambina in holy matrimony."

Morovich moved into the seat behind his quarry. His men stood in the aisle, a little to the rear of the church.

Woody and Harry looked around. It was hopeless. Then Natalia stood up.

"I wish to speak," she said.

The priest lowered his book and looked up. Every head, including those of the bride and groom, turned to the rear.

"Yes?" the priest said.

"This man," Natalia said loudly, pointing to the groom, "is already married!"

Harry smiled. Woody looked puzzled. Every guest in the church gasped.

"Married to whom?" the priest asked.

"To me!" Natalia cried.

The groom looked stunned. "What is this?" he asked. "I've never seen her before in my life!"

"Come home, Pietro!" Natalia said, sobbing. "Please. If not for me, then for the sake of the children!"

The bride burst into tears. She ran from the altar and into the arms of her parents.

"You are lying!" the groom shouted. "She is nothing but a liar!"

"I wish that were so," Natalia wailed. "But little Pietro cries for his father!"

The groom came storming down the aisle. He had murder in his eyes.

"You will leave here at once!" he said.

"I will not," Natalia said quietly. "Uncle Luigi and I have come to take you home."

"I will throw you out myself!" the groom bellowed.

"Don't lay a hand on me!" Natalia shouted.

"Who will stop me?"

"Uncle Luigi!" she said, pointing at Morovich.

The groom leaped for Uncle Luigi. His men came rushing to the rescue. Several of the groom's friends and relatives came rushing to *his* rescue.

Natalia slid along the bench to the side aisle. Harry and Woody followed. The Russians were now somewhere near the bottom of a pile of men in the center aisle.

Natalia slipped out the side door unseen. Woody and Harry slipped out behind her. They made their way through some back streets to Harry's waiting car.

Harry (James Hampton) offers his comic book writer friend Woody (Michael Crawford) a soothing cup of tea, and a lot of advice, after his leap off the Eiffel Tower.

Dressed for his role as Secret Agent Condorman,
Woody leaves for Istanbul on a job for the
U.S. Government.

Natalia (Barbara Carrera), the beautiful Russian spy, arrives for her meeting with Woody.

The secret papers are safe in Woody's briefcase, which (*below*) connects with the jaw of an enemy agent as he makes his getaway.

Harry and his boss, Russ Devlin (Dana Elcar), ask Woody to take on another job: Get Natalia out of the clutches of her Russian spy boss, Krokov (Oliver Reed).

With the push of a button, Woody turns his gypsy caravan into a sleek racing car and pulls away from his evil pursuers— the *Brochnoviatch.*

When his trick launching pad fails to stop the *Brochnoviatch*, Woody heads for the water and floats away—his Condorcar becomes a hydrofoil.

Krokov will stop at nothing to keep Natalia from defecting to the West.

Disguised as a policeman, Harry gets Woody and Natalia out of jail, but (*below*) it's not so easy to get out of the handcuffs.

Condorman crashes the party for rich oil sheiks at the Russian villa in Monte Carlo.

Woody and Natalia make their escape off the roof
of the villa while Harry distracts the Russians with
a few well-timed bombs.

After a scorching race to freedom in their laser-gun ship, Woody, Natalia, and Harry return to America, where Woody introduces Natalia to baseball.

This time Krokov was being much calmer about the failure to apprehend the two fugitives, and Morovich didn't like it a bit. Krokov sat at his desk, leaning back in his swivel chair. He kept casting glances at the contents of a large folder he held in his lap.

Morovich was holding a pointer to a map of northern Italy on Krokov's wall. His face was covered with bruises and his left hand was heavily bandaged. These souvenirs of the lost battle in the church didn't do his morale any good. Perhaps they were responsible for the slight smile that Krokov couldn't seem to keep hidden.

"We can't be sure of their whereabouts,"

Morovich was saying, as he pointed to the map, "but we think they are headed toward—"

"The Alps?" Krokov said, not even bothering to hide the smile.

Morovich paused, jolted by the interruption. He took a few seconds to control his anger, then went on.

"Yes, that's what we suspect. If we are correct, they could cross at any number of places." He moved the pointer as he spoke. "St. Bernard Pass. Near Mont Blanc. Below the—"

"I know precisely where they will cross," Krokov said.

"You do?" Morovich said. The tip of the pointer slid to the floor.

"The best-kept secrets of Woodrow Wilkins," Krokov said laughing, "can be had for a tiny coin."

Krokov stood up and put the folder on the desk. He took a comic book from inside the folder and waved it at Morovich.

"Here is a truck," he said, holding out a page, "that becomes a racing car..." He riffled to another page. "A car that becomes a boat...exotic weapons...exploding rockets ...It's all here, my dear Morovich, including—"

He held another comic book up for inspection.

their room, Harry started taking off his shoes.

"Oh, boy!" he said. "I can feel that hot shower now!" Then he looked at Natalia and his gentleman's conscience got the better of him. "Of course, I could always feel it later," he said.

"No," she said, smiling. "It is all yours."

He made a dash for the bathroom. Woody fell onto the bed and closed his eyes.

"Just five minutes," he said sleepily. "A quick nap is all I need. Just..."

He was asleep before he finished. Natalia listened to the sound of the shower and smiled at Woody.

She walked toward the balcony to take in the beauty of the mountains. The group of children gathered on the sidewalk below seemed to have grown even larger. When she stepped onto the balcony one of them pointed. All the others looked up.

Natalia looked down at the children, and they began to wave. *What is going on?* she wondered. This did not look like the treatment given to tourists — even in the off-season.

She stepped back inside and stood thoughtfully for a moment. Then she left the room and went downstairs. She went outside and walked across the street to the children.

They huddled together, and some of them giggled. Natalia waited. Finally, one of the boys became brave enough to speak.

"You *are* her, aren't you?" the boy asked.

"Of course it's her," another boy said.

"It is!" a girl said. "It really is!"

Gently, Natalia asked, "What is this, children? Why do you keep staring at me?"

An older boy, who seemed to be entranced, chanted "The Empress of Space, Time, and Beauty."

That wasn't much help. Natalia watched him as he reached inside his jacket and pulled out a comic book. He held it out to her.

"Laser Lady!" he said.

Natalia took the book from him. The cover drawing of Laser Lady took her breath away. She opened to the first page and saw another full-page drawing of herself. She thumbed through the book and saw dozens more.

She turned back to the first page, and her eye traveled to the bottom. "Published by Woodrow Wilkins Enterprises," she read.

She was dizzy and still having trouble breathing. A little girl tugged at her sleeve and seemed to speak from a great distance.

"How did you get to be Laser Lady?" the girl asked.

Natalia looked again at the cover of the comic book. *What is this all about?* she wondered.

"Natalia!" It was Harry's voice. She turned to see him run up to her, his shirt still only half-buttoned. The children scampered away as he approached.

"Natalia!" he said, nearly out of breath. "You scared the life out of me! I come out of the shower, you're gone, and Woody's out like a light. I figured they'd grabbed you!"

He noticed that she wasn't really hearing him. She looked as though she'd just had a terrible shock.

"Natalia?" he said softly. "Are you all right?"

"Yes," Natalia whispered. She seemed to be just waking up. "Yes, I'm all right. Harry? Who are you?"

"Are you sure you're all right?" Harry asked. "What do you mean, who am I?"

"Woody is Condorman," she said. "I am Laser Lady. Who are you?"

Now that he understood what she meant, he relaxed a bit. "You know?" he asked.

She held the comic book up.

"Oh," Harry said. "Let's take a walk."

She handed the book back to its owner. Then

she let Harry take her arm and lead her down the street. The children watched them go off.

"You had to find out sooner or later," Harry said, "but for Woody's sake, I kept quiet. This...this huge lie is not his fault, Natalia. I got him into it. I sent him to Istanbul. Talked him into Yugoslavia. You must have guessed by now that he isn't a real agent. But locked inside him, there really is a lunatic cloak-and-dagger guy. His imagination is his weapon. So now you know what he is—a modern knight, fighting enemy dragons for the love of a beautiful woman in distress."

Natalia stared silently at the mountains. Finally she took a deep breath and said, "So he's living in a dream?"

"Dream?" Harry said. "It's *real* to him. If you wake him, it would destroy him. Natalia, he's doing all this for you. If he thought for a second that you knew—"

"I won't tell, Harry."

Harry stopped walking and faced her. "He loves you, lady. I don't want to see him get hurt."

"Neither do I," she said softly.

There was nothing to do until the following morning. So after dinner at the inn, Harry and

Woody and Natalia stayed downstairs for the singing and dancing.

Harry had made up his mind to dance with every girl in the village. He was now into his second hour of nonstop movement, and he wasn't showing any signs of letting up.

Woody and Natalia sat at a table and watched. They'd had their fill of dancing long before. Woody liked to stare at Natalia's face, so he'd voted for sitting instead of dancing. He watched her let out a deep sigh.

"A ruble for your thoughts," he said.

She smiled at him. "I was just thinking," she said, "about Paris. Soon we will be there."

"Yes," Woody said. "Another couple of days."

"Then will come the meetings," she said, "the interrogations. Probably trips to Washington. And finally, a new identity in a new land."

"Finally," Woody said.

She looked at him in silence for a moment. He wondered what kinds of things she wasn't telling him, might never tell him. He wondered if knowing would make any difference to him. He thought not.

"Woody," she said, and he leaned closer. "When I parted from Krokov, I made a vow to myself. I promised I would never again love a man who lived a life of deception. But now, now I think that there is deception and there is *deception*."

Woody's forehead wrinkled. "I don't understand," he said.

"No," she said laughing, "but I do! When I get to America and start reading the Sunday funnies, eating my Big Mac, and planning for the senior prom —"

"Well," he laughed, "you may have missed the prom."

"I would like it very much," she said, "if I could pick up my American telephone, call my friend Woody, and say, 'Come over and be democratic with me.'"

He grinned and said, "I'll bring the dip if you'll bring the Dostoevski."

She looked at him tenderly, but she seemed to have no idea what he meant.

"It's just a joke," he said, staring into her eyes. "It means yes."

As they stared at each other the music swelled, leading to a finale. Woody didn't hear it. When he spoke, it was as though the two of them were alone at the top of the Matterhorn.

"I think I'm in love with you," he murmured.

Natalia leaned forward and yelled, "What? I didn't hear what you said."

At that instant the music stopped. Woody shouted into the suddenly silent room, "I think I'm in love with you!"

There was a burst of cheering from the floor. Woody and Natalia, realizing it was for them, stood and acknowledged the applause.

Then Natalia took Woody's face in her hands and gave him a soft, lingering kiss. The crowd cheered and the music began again.

Three brightly dressed figures trudged through the snow, squinting in the bright morning sunlight. Their destination was a ski station just above the base of the mountain. They'd left the inn before dawn, mostly to avoid running into Natalia's fan club again. Woody's plan didn't allow for spectators.

He stood on a bank of snow and helped Harry, then Natalia, climb up and join him.

"Where are we going?" Natalia asked.

"There," Woody said, pointing further up.

They looked up to see the deserted ski station only a few hundred yards away. Woody resumed climbing, and they followed.

"That's our first-class ticket to Switzerland!" he called over his shoulder.

When they reached the station, Woody examined the cable that led up the mountain. Then he went to the door of the station and pushed. The door didn't budge.

"Harry," Woody said, annoyed, "the plan called for this door to be left open."

Harry, still winded from the climb, said, "Tell you the truth, Woody, I only handled the jail escape. Russ handled the snow. Let me try. Maybe it's just frozen stuck."

Harry pushed on the door with his shoulder. Nothing. He backed off a few feet, took a step, and pushed again.

Then he went a few feet farther away and tried a third time. He threw all his weight at the door. There was a loud, splintering noise, and the door flew open. Harry flew into the room, hit the opposite wall, and fell to the floor, groaning.

He rolled over and grabbed his shoulder. "Ohhh!" he moaned. "I've broken my back before we even got started!"

Woody stepped over him and surveyed the room. "Look for a tall box!" he said excitedly.

He and Natalia began poking around — under tables, behind doors, and up on shelves.

Harry realized he wasn't going to get any sympathy from them. He slowly got on his feet and helped them search.

"Here!" Natalia said. She stepped aside to reveal a tall cardboard box inside a locker. Woody rushed over and dragged it out.

"I think this is it!" he said, tearing the box open.

"I hope that's it!" Harry said. "Though I have no idea what *it* is!"

Woody got the box open and pulled out three metal rods, each about ten feet long, with a roller on top, a handlebar in the center, and a footrest near the bottom. Just below each footrest was a small pair of tanks with nozzles on them.

"Good guy, Russ!" Woody said, beaming. "He got it exactly right!"

"He did?" Harry said, scratching his head.

"What are they, Woody?" Natalia asked.

"I'd rather show you than tell you," Woody said.

They helped him carry the rods outside to the platform near the cable. Woody picked up one of the rods and handed it to Natalia. He held the second one out to Harry. Harry kept his hands at his sides, waiting to hear just what was going to be expected of him.

"It's really very simple," Woody said. "They're jet rods. You just put the rollers on the cable like this..."

He stepped forward and fitted the roller onto the cable. Then he put one foot on the footrest.

"You climb on like this..."

He swung his other foot up and grasped the handlebars with both hands.

"And when you're ready to go," he said happily, "you just hit this button and zowie—right up the mountain!"

"WAIT A SECOND!" Harry screamed. His voice echoed off the mountains. "Hold on! Everybody out of the pool! Stop the clock, and whoa! You want me to climb on that jet-powered pogo stick and go up that mountain?"

"Do you have a better idea?" Woody asked.

"Yeah," Harry said angrily. "What do you say we wait here for the big thaw? Then we can just walk over!"

"Harry!" Woody said. "There's nothing to be afraid of!"

"Oh, yeah! What if we fall? I have this neurotic thing about death, you know! Five feet out on that thing and I'll let go and call for Mama! No way, Woody old boy! I can't handle heights!"

Woody hesitated for only a beat. Then he said reassuringly, "No sweat, Harry. You come with me. I'll hold you and we'll go first. That way we'll be there to catch Natalia."

Woody held out his hand to Harry.

"Who'll be there to catch me?" Harry whimpered.

"Just keep your eyes closed, Harry," Natalia said, gently pushing him toward Woody. "And don't look down. I'll press the button."

Woody held on to the handlebar and Harry stepped up behind him. He wrapped his arms around Woody and stepped onto the footrest.

With his eyes closed tight, he asked, "But couldn't I just—"

"No!" Natalia said, leaning forward and pressing the button.

He watched them take off like a shot, zooming up the side of the mountain. Then she quickly slipped her own rod onto the cable, stepped on, pressed the button, and took off after them.

The faint sound of Natalia's and Woody's laughter could be heard from far off. Krokov could hear it as he stood on the platform at the opposite end of the cable, watching them through binoculars.

"Do you see them?" he said into his walkie-talkie.

"Yes!" said the voice of Morovich.

He was stationed at the base of the mountain, watching through the sight of a high-powered rifle. He aimed first at Natalia, itching to pull the trigger. Then he moved the sight until it was trained on his assigned target. He aimed for the roller that held Woody and Harry to the cable.

Krokov watched for a few more seconds. Then he spat his order into the walkie-talkie: "Now!"

The single shot drowned out the tiny sounds of laughter. It echoed against the mountains as Natalia watched the roller in front of her fall apart. She saw Woody and Harry fall through the air, hit the ground, and sink into the snow.

She gripped the rod tightly as the mountain rushed below her at great speed. She turned to look through her tears. All she could see was two gaping holes in the white snow.

Tears streamed down her face as she swooped onto the platform. She kicked and swung her arms, but two strong men grabbed her and held her still. Krokov's evil smile greeted her.

The sound of her crying was loud, now that

the echo of the rifle shot had died down. The men dragged her to a helicopter and tossed her inside. They climbed in after her. Krokov followed.

Now the sound of the rising helicopter tore the silence of the mountains to shreds. Natalia looked down at the holes in the snow, then collapsed into a sobbing ball.

Morovich was in his car the instant the two targets had hit the snow. He paused only long enough to see Natalia arrive at the platform, where Krokov was waiting, then took off to meet them.

The helicopter was gone when a deep groan came from one of the craters in the snow. The groan slowly formed itself into a man's name.

"Harry?" There was a long pause. "Harry?"

"Spare me, Woody" came from the other crater. "Please spare me."

Woody's face appeared over the edge of his crater.

"Harry," he said. "I think they're gone. We can move now.

"Speak...for...yourself," Harry moaned. "I ... may ... never ... move ... again."

Natalia's face was buried in the pillow, which was still damp from her tears. She had slept most of the night, but never more than twenty minutes at a time. Krokov stood watching her arms twitch as she mumbled in her sleep.

He walked over to the floor-to-ceiling window and yanked at the cord. The heavy drapes flew open, filling the room with Monte Carlo sunlight.

Natalia stirred, turned over on her back, and slowly opened her eyes. Krokov sat on the edge of the bed and smiled smugly at her.

"Good morning, Natalia," he said with some

amusement in his voice. "I trust you slept well?"

She turned her face away from him.

"You didn't really think I'd let you get away, did you?" he said. "After all you've meant to me?"

She turned to face him and raised herself on her elbows. "I hate you!" she hissed, and fell back on the pillow.

"Yes," he said, smirking. "And I would have enjoyed seeing you killed. You don't know how tempted I was."

"I wish you had done it," she said, her eyes closed. "It would have been better than this."

She sniffled, then began to sob.

"Save your tears," he said harshly. "I am going to keep you alive. Our story will be that you only pretended to defect in order to capture this Condorman."

She opened her eyes and glared at him. He smiled in return.

"Dear Morovich," he went on, "will have to take the blame for the failure of the mission. Of course, he will have to be killed. We wouldn't want the Party to hear his side of the story, would we?"

She glared at him with pure hatred. "You pig!" she said. "Do you really think things will ever be the same between us again?"

"At the moment," he said calmly, "I won't worry about that. Just remember one thing, my dear. Whatever happens in the future, it will be preferable to a slow death in a Siberian work camp."

He reached out and smoothed her hair. She spun away and moved to the opposite edge of the bed.

"Don't touch me!"

In a flash of anger, he raised his hand to slap her. Then he lowered it, regained his composure, and smiled again.

"Very well, Natalia. But for the time being, everything between us will appear as normal. You will play the role of the perfect hostess. The oil ministers will be arriving tomorrow. I want you up and about, and looking your best. You will laugh and joke with them and make sure they are happy."

She was staring at the ceiling. Krokov seemed disappointed that she wasn't responding.

"Oh, and one other thing," he said. "If you have any ideas of escaping, please forget them. This cozy villa is a fortress, and your every move will be watched."

Through clenched teeth, she said, "Get out of here!"

"Ah," he said, going to the door, "that's

better. It's your fighting spirit that has always attracted me."

Krokov opened the door and stood in the doorway. Natalia was staring at the ceiling again.

"I will leave you now," he said. "Prepare yourself to make up for what you have done. And darling, no more trouble. One wrong move, and I will kill you on the spot!"

He closed the door gently behind him and walked down the carpeted hall. Morovich was waiting for him at the head of the stairs.

"Any news?" Krokov asked.

"No," Morovich said glumly. "The first reports have been confirmed. No sign of any bodies."

Krokov stared at him and raised his eyebrows. Morovich flushed.

"But they *must* be dead!" Morovich said. "I *saw* them fall!"

"Yes," Krokov said, smirking. "Nevertheless, I think we need to take some precautions. Prepare them now."

He turned and hurried down the stairs. Morovich took a deep breath before responding.

"Yes, Comrade Commissar," he said, his lip curling just a bit.

* * *

Woody stood again on the balcony of the little inn at the foot of the Matterhorn. He stared at the famous mountain. He had lost Natalia up there. What was he going to do to get her back?

Harry stepped out from the room and they stared together in silence for a few seconds. Then Harry turned to him.

"I just spoke to Russ, Woody."

"Does he know anything?"

"Natalia's safe," Harry said. "She's playing hostess for Krokov at the Russian villa in Monte Carlo."

Woody's eyes widened. "We have to get her out of there!" he said.

"No," Harry said quietly. "We have orders to report back to Paris. The mission is officially a bust."

"I can't go back!" Woody said, grabbing Harry's arm. "Not without Natalia. Harry, I love her."

Harry put his arm around his friend. "I know that, Woody," he said. "But what can we do about it?"

"They gave me Top Red Clearance," Woody said. "I still have it. That gets me anything I need, including Fort Knox."

"That was before we were ordered back to Paris," Harry said sadly.

"Forget the order!" Woody said, going back into the room. "Tell them you didn't see me in time."

"I can't do that, Woody," Harry said, following him back inside.

"What do you mean, *can't?*" Woody yelled. He turned and scowled at his friend. "Did *I* say *can't* when you asked me to go to Istanbul? Or Yugoslavia? Now suddenly you're worried about *rules?* With Natalia maybe gone forever!"

"Well—" Harry said sheepishly.

"Harry, please," Woody said, calming down. "Just two more days. That's all I ask. It's killing me to think of Natalia as Krokov's prisoner."

"All right," Harry said decisively, bringing a grin to Woody's face. "We *do* owe you at least that much for what we've put you through."

Woody threw his arms around Harry and kissed him loudly on the cheek.

"Harry!" he sang. "Harry, you're beautiful!"

"Hey, cool it!" Harry said, disentangling himself. "We have work to do. We still have to figure out a plan."

"Are you kidding?" Woody said. "What do you think I've been doing since we climbed out of that snow?"

"I hesitate to ask this," Harry said. "But what do you have in mind, Woody old pal?"

"Nothing too elaborate," Woody said, grinning. "The main prop is a great ... big ... beautiful ... yacht!"

It took only thirty-six hours to get the fully equipped prop into position. That Top Red Clearance is magic, Woody decided.

When the yacht anchored in the harbor, Krokov viewed it through a high-powered telescope from his balcony. His aide, Vito, who had made the discovery, stood beside him.

"You're right, Vito," Krokov said. "It is indeed interesting."

Vito looked pleased with himself as Krokov studied the activity on the yacht. What he saw was a bearded Arab sheik, in traditional white robes, lounging on a deck chair. Several men and women, all in traditional Arab dress, bowed and scraped before him.

As high-powered as the telescope was, though, it could give Krokov only a general idea of what was going on aboard the yacht. That was fine with Woody, who stretched out on the deck chair and accepted a bunch of grapes from a nearby servant.

Woody popped a grape into his mouth and smiled up at another bearded sheik, motioning him to a lounge chair beside his.

"Sit down, Harry," he said. "Have a grape."

Harry sat, but refused the grape that Woody held out to him. "Woody," he said worriedly, "maybe we should slow down a little. When Russ sees the bill for all this he's going to deport us. I just keep asking myself, *where to?*"

Woody offered the grapes to the servant, who took a handful. "Harry, Harry, Harry," he said cheerfully. "We have to make a big impression. We'd never convince them with a canoe and two paddles."

"Woody," Harry said, "we don't even know for sure that anyone will notice us at all."

"Trust me," Woody said, popping another grape. "They'll notice. Just take a look at page five over there."

Woody gestured to a table between the two deck chairs. Harry opened the sketchbook on the table and flipped through the pages. Page five showed a drawing of the Monte Carlo Casino.

Later that night, Harry learned that Woody's drawing on page five was faithful in the smallest detail to the real thing. He also learned something about gambling. He learned it was a good way to set yourself up for a heart attack.

He watched Woody using huge sums of the department's money to help with the "big impression," and acting as though he were playing with Monopoly money.

Only one thing saved Harry from that heart attack. Woody happened to be winning.

While Woody was cleaning up at a table in the back, Krokov came strolling in through the main entrance, accompanied by a woman. Vito and another woman walked behind them.

Just inside the entrance they stopped to look things over. Krokov smiled.

"Vito," he said, "it looks as though our Arab friends are out in force tonight. I want a complete list of all sheiks seen gambling. It may be useful to us at another time."

"Yes, Comrade Commissar," Vito said, jotting down names in a small notebook.

They continued on into the main casino. At the sound of loud applause, they stopped. A cheering crowd was clapping loudly for two bearded Arab sheiks, followed by a train of servants, who were marching toward them.

Each sheik carried two briefcases, and Krokov had no doubt that the cases were filled with money. The sheiks stopped and waved to the well-wishers. Then they marched past Krokov and Vito, followed by the servants.

As they went out the door, Krokov motioned to a man standing near one of the tables. The man came over, and Krokov spoke to him.

"What happened, Henri?"

"Amazing, my dear Sergei," Henri said. "Simply amazing. This Arab — he took the house to its limit."

"And what is that?" Krokov asked.

"Two million francs!" Henri exclaimed, returning to his spot at the gambling table.

Krokov and Vito walked outside, followed by the two women. They watched the two sheiks get into a Rolls-Royce.

When the car pulled away, Krokov said, "Vito, who is that man?"

"He is the sheik from the yacht, Comrade Commissar. Mujibub Amat Fasad. He is the Grand Exalted Emir of Mahirahn."

"Mahirahn?" Krokov asked.

"Ten square miles of oil," Vito said, "covered by a thin layer of sand."

"And this is the first we've heard of him?" Krokov said incredulously.

Vito looked very pleased at the prospect of being able to answer his superior's questions. He nodded slightly.

"According to the underground," he said, "the man was nothing more than another desert wanderer. Then several months ago he struck oil. Now he is the seventh richest man in the world."

"Really?" Krokov said, staring at the glowing taillights of the Rolls. "See that he is at the party tomorrow."

Vito was known for his efficiency. That was how he'd become Krokov's Monte Carlo aide. Because of that efficiency, Woody and Harry stood at a cocktail party inside the villa the next afternoon.

Harry slid around the room, trying not to have to talk to anyone. To keep himself busy, he tried estimating the total net worth of the people in the room. He decided it was enough to run several small countries for three or four years.

Woody was getting more pleasure out of his role-playing. He moved from one group of people to another, pretending to be interested in whatever it was they were talking about.

Being here was a mixture of delicious relief and unbearable tension for Woody. The relief came from seeing Natalia. She was with Krokov, making her own rounds from one group to another.

The tension came from trying to figure out how to get to her.

"Of course," a businessman was saying to Woody, "our North Sea oil will make a difference. But the question remains, can we produce it in sufficient quantity?"

Woody was craning his neck, trying to get a glimpse of Natalia at her current spot. The businessman shifted his feet, and Woody found himself staring right into his face.

"Do you see that as a problem in the long run?" the man asked him.

"Huh?" Woody said. "Oh! Well, that all depends. There's the long run and the short run. And...uh...what was your question again?"

Annoyed, the man repeated slowly, "Do you think our North Sea will produce enough oil?"

"The North Sea?" Woody said, suddenly

slipping back into his spy character. "Hah! Enough for a small salad, I'd say. Nothing more."

The man's eyes widened, and he opened his mouth, ready to argue. Woody, keeping his eye on Natalia, figured it was time to move on.

"Excuse me," he said. "Business calls. I'm closing a deal for Rhode Island."

He went gliding across the floor, his robes flowing behind him. As he went out to the terrace, he was followed by another gliding sheik.

"Everything is set," Harry whispered. "Have you talked to her yet?"

"I can't get near her," Woody whispered angrily. "Every time I turn around somebody tries to sell me something."

"Well, whatever you do," Harry said, "don't buy. When are you going to make your move?"

Looking out into the garden, Woody said, "Right now."

Krokov and Natalia had just come outside with two men. Now Krokov and the two men were moving away, talking quietly. Natalia was alone.

"Give me five minutes," Woody whispered. "Then let it go."

"Five minutes," Harry said, looking at his watch. "You got it."

Natalia was staring out at the water as Woody approached her from behind. She turned when he spoke loudly.

"A most beautiful place, Monaco," he said in his best Mahirahnian accent.

She composed her hostess smile and turned to her guest. "Yes, it is," she said. "I don't believe we've met."

In his normal voice, Woody said, "Don't say anything. The cavalry has arrived."

He peeled a bit of his beard from his face and winked at her. She was about to scream, but Woody clasped his hand over her mouth until the urge was gone.

"Woody!" she gasped. "They told me you were dead! Krokov! If he knew, he would kill you in a moment!"

Woody waited a few seconds for her fear to subside. Then he said softly, "I came to get you."

Natalia looked over Woody's shoulder. Krokov was still talking with the two men, but he kept glancing at Natalia and the sheik. Woody watched her face harden before she spoke.

"No," she said coldly. "I cannot go with you."

"What do you mean?" Woody said, astounded. This was the last thing he expected.

"I'm sorry," she said, turning and looking out at the water again. "I've changed my mind."

Even inside the robes, Woody suddenly looked deflated. His face was twisted with confusion and anger.

"Changed your mind?" he repeated. Then he lowered his voice to a safer level. "Are you crazy? This isn't like deciding what to have for dinner! This is defection!"

Natalia turned to face him. She saw Krokov coming toward them.

"It's Krokov!" she whispered, terrified.

"Forget Krokov!" Woody said. "Come with me!"

"No!" she said. "Krokov had a plan. Don't you understand? You aren't that stupid, are you?"

Woody's head was spinning. Her voice sounded like ringing steel. Did she really call him stupid just now?

"He thought you were a top American agent," she said mockingly. "My defection was a trick — to kidnap you. Of course, now we know that you are merely a foolish dreamer who draws comic books—not worth the bullet it would take to kill you."

Woody was speechless. He wouldn't have

believed she could look that ugly, sneering at him the way she was.

"So go!" she said under her breath. "Please! And don't try to—"

"So!" Krokov said approvingly. "I see you have met the sheik."

He joined them, smiling like the charming host he was. Natalia offered a smile in response to his.

"Yes," she said lightly. "He thought we had met before."

"Is that so?" Krokov said, just as lightly.

"It seems I was mistaken," Woody said, staring into her eyes. "A foolish dream perhaps."

Natalia took Krokov's arm, and they slowly walked past Woody. He stared out at the water.

"It was a pleasure meeting you," she said. "I'm sorry we didn't have more time to chat. Perhaps some other time."

Woody wanted to fling something at her. Then he heard her parting remark.

"If you bring the dip," she called out, "I'll bring the Dostoevski!"

Woody had two mind-crushing thoughts at that instant. The first was that Natalia had just given him a secret signal. That parting remark told him she hadn't meant everything else she'd said.

The second was that his five minutes were up. The explosion that rocked the villa told him that Harry was carrying out his part of the plan.

_____ *12*

Woody had no time for thinking, so he acted instead. Natalia was lying on the ground, along with a dozen other people. Krokov was crouched under a table with his back to her.

Woody ran through pieces of glass and brick and grabbed Natalia's arm. As she got to her feet, Krokov looked up and saw what was happening.

Still shaken from the blast, Krokov teetered toward them. Woody, pulling Natalia behind him, rushed Krokov and pushed him back to the ground. Then he led Natalia into the building.

On the other side of the house, Harry

emerged from the smoke that enveloped the front door. He stepped right into the arms of Morovich and his three burly men.

"A mad terrorist!" Harry exclaimed, hoping his beard was still on straight. "Around the back, quick!"

The Russians hurried toward the back with their guns drawn. Harry hopped into the Rolls-Royce standing in the driveway and started it up.

Krokov was back on his feet, surrounded by six guards. He looked through a window and saw Woody and Natalia heading up a stairway.

"After them!" he screamed, and the guards obeyed.

The front gate was open, but two armed guards stood in the center to stop anyone from leaving. As Harry neared them, they began waving their arms for him to stop.

Harry pressed down on the accelerator. When the guards saw what he had in mind, they jumped to the side.

Roaring through the gate, Harry sang out, "Oh, Russ, if you could only see me now!"

Natalia and Woody reached the top of the second staircase and heard the guards right behind them. Natalia stopped, hoisted a large potted palm, and flung it at them.

112

It crashed in the middle of the staircase, sending the guards scattering for safety. Woody grabbed her hand and led her to the final flight of stairs.

"Wait!" she protested. "Where are we going? Why are we doing this?"

"You tell me," he said, panting. "*You* just knocked out a couple of guards. Five minutes ago you were singing 'Sickles and Soviets Forever.' "

"Woody," she said, her eyes beginning to moisten.

"You want out?" he said.

"I want you," she answered tenderly.

"Then point me to the roof!" he said.

"This way!" She grabbed his hand and led him up the stairs. As they ran into the attic, Krokov and the guards reached the top of the stairs.

"There they are!" Krokov yelled.

Woody slammed the door and looked around the attic. The heaviest thing he could see was a large dresser near the door. They slid it across the floor until it was blocking the door.

They ran up a small flight of stairs and out onto the roof. Woody hurried to the edge and looked out. There was Harry in the Rolls, barreling along toward the pier. So far, so good.

They could hear the pounding at the attic

door. Natalia came to the edge and looked down.

"Woody," she said shakily, "I'm frightened!"

"Don't worry," he said, tearing off his beard and his headdress. "Condorman has it all figured out."

She looked down again at the drop of more than a hundred feet. "We're trapped, Woody!"

"Don't you believe it!" he said, pulling off his shoes.

"How are we going to escape?" she shrieked. *Fly?*

He stopped what he was doing and looked at her, disappointed. "I was hoping to surprise you," he said.

He pulled away his robe and let it fall to his feet. He stood there, beaming in his Condorman suit as footsteps pounded into the attic.

"You're not serious!" Natalia said as he stood on the edge of the roof.

Woody extended his arms and Condorman's wings flapped into position.

"Get behind me!" Woody yelled. "And hold on tight!"

The guards had reached the locked roof door. Natalia heard Krokov ordering one of them to shoot the lock. She stepped behind

Woody, put her arms around his waist, and closed her eyes.

Woody took off as a shot destroyed the lock on the door. Krokov and his men rushed out on the roof. Nothing. Then they heard Natalia's scream.

They ran to the edge and looked down. They watched Condorman and Laser Lady plunge toward the ground.

Woody desperately fought for control of his wings. Less than ten feet from the ground he won the battle. They sailed back up and over the wall of the compound.

The guards fired their pistols, but Condorman was too far away to be damaged. Krokov held his clenched fists out in front of him.

Then he turned to one of the guards. "Call Morovich. Tell him to prepare them."

Natalia had opened her eyes by now. She watched, with Woody, as Harry made his way through narrow streets to the harbor.

"I can't hold on much longer!" she yelled in Woody's ear. "When are we going to land?"

"As soon as Harry gets to the meeting spot!" he yelled over his shoulder.

He adjusted the wings to keep them circling. They watched Harry screech to a halt on the dock and fly out of the car.

He patted it on the hood for a job well done. Then he ran to the gangplank leading to the yacht.

As Harry got on board the yacht, Woody looked out at the road his friend had just taken. Three cars full of Russians were tearing along in their direction.

Harry waved up to them from the yacht and Woody began his descent. A loud snapping sound made Natalia tighten her grip on his midsection.

"Woody! What's happening?"

"Just a minor technical problem!"

"What is it?" she yelled.

"The wings are falling off!"

Their return to earth was faster than the plan called for. Harry got out of their way just in time.

As they fell toward the yacht, Woody began flapping the huge wings, trying to slow down their descent. It didn't help.

They came racing onto the deck, feet first, wings extended. Natalia lost her hold on Woody and toppled backwards. He kept going, now running, now hopping, now sailing for a few feet. Finally he fell to a complete stop.

Natalia and Harry ran up to him and helped

him out of his wings. Then they ran to the side of the yacht to make their way down a rope ladder.

"Why did you come and get me?" Natalia asked as Harry hopped over the side.

"Why did you pretend you didn't want to come?" Woody asked, pushing her toward the rope ladder.

"I couldn't let you be discovered and killed," she answered, following Harry. "If I'd told you the truth you would have tried something stupid."

Harry's voice rose from below. "Instead of this sane and sensible thing we're doing now?"

Harry was standing in a motorboat, waiting to help Natalia get in. Woody got on the ladder and followed Natalia.

All three of them stood in the boat, which was covered front and back with canvas. Woody held Natalia as Harry removed the canvas coverings.

"But how do you feel about my being 'a foolish dreamer who draws comic books'?" Woody said.

"Did I say that?" Natalia asked innocently.

"You did."

"Well," she said grinning, "Laser Lady will say anything to save the man she loves."

She leaned forward and kissed him. They could hear cars screeching to a stop on the pier behind the Rolls.

Harry started up the motor, and Natalia looked around at the boat. Not long ago, she would have been dumbfounded by the sight of this All-Purpose, Jet-Powered, Super-Hydra-Plane, or whatever she was in. But now, she was getting used to Woody's "comic-book" inventions.

From the villa Krokov watched Woody's boat take off. Without looking up from the telescope, he said, "Now!"

Morovich walked over to a radio transmitter. He repeated the order into a microphone.

The result of the order took a few seconds to make itself apparent out on the bay. Harry was piloting the speedboat away from Monte Carlo and whooping like a crazed cowboy.

"We beat 'em, baby!" he yelled.

The whine behind them made Woody turn. He saw the four boats closing in on theirs.

"Not yet, we haven't," he shouted to Harry.

Natalia turned and saw the four black racers behind them. Woody moved to the rear of the boat.

"The Brochnoviatch!" Natalia said.

Woody pressed a button in the side of the

boat. A hatch opened and a strange-looking cannon slid out of the floor. It raised itself and locked into position. Woody climbed into the gunner's seat and patted the cannon.

"I was afraid I wouldn't get to try this one," he said grinning.

"What is it?" Natalia yelled over the roar of the motor.

Woody laughed and answered, "You haven't been reading your Laser Lady!"

He flipped a switch on the cannon and began to aim it at the oncoming boats. The gun whirred and pulsated. A light began to flow from its opening—first yellow, then blue, then a fiery red. The whirring became a high-pitched shriek.

They saw hatches opening on the sides of each of the Brochnoviatch boats. Eight rocket launchers were aimed directly at them. But Woody's laser cannon was too fast and too much for them. One by one he aimed the light at each boat. One by one the boats were consumed in flames.

Harry cheered and Natalia threw her arms around Woody's neck and kissed him.

"Head for the airport, Harry!" Woody called out. "We're going home!" He put his arms around Natalia and returned the kiss.

"Oh, no!" Harry gasped. "I hate to break anything up," he yelled, "but we're in trouble!"

He pointed off to the side. In the distance another boat was coming at them. It, too, was huge and black. But it made the other Brochnoviatch boats look like toys.

Krokov was piloting this boat, with Morovich at his side. In spite of the distance between the two boats, Woody, Natalia, and Harry knew the two faces in the black boat had hatred written on them.

"To the cove, Harry!" Woody ordered as he hopped back into the gunner's seat.

As Krokov's rockets whizzed by them, Woody trained his laser light on their pursuers. But Krokov was better at evasive action than any of his skilled drivers.

Woody managed to hit one of the two rocket launchers and put it out of commission, but Krokov was back on course in seconds, firing the rockets from the other launcher.

Woody turned to see that they were near the cove. Overhead was the helicopter called for in his plan.

He turned back to his target and fired, just as Krokov launched another rocket at him. The laser hit the rocket launcher and destroyed it, sending the black boat off on a veering course. At almost the same instant the rocket grazed the tip of Woody's laser-cannon, jolting him out of his seat.

He hopped back in and fired again. Nothing happened. His weapon was gone.

Harry pulled into a tiny cove, and the helicopter began descending toward them. Woody looked back to see that the black boat was chasing again. But now Morovich was piloting it.

He was headed straight for them. He had only one thing in mind—to smash his boat into theirs, killing everyone.

As the hooks were lowered from the helicopter, Krokov fought to get the wheel. But Morovich pushed him out of the way and continued into the cove at ever-increasing speed.

Harry fastened a hook to one side of the boat. Woody and Natalia fastened the hook on the opposite side. Morovich was less than a hundred yards from them now. It was too late for him even to slow down.

Krokov leaped over the side of the boat. As he bobbed in the water, he could see Woody's boat being lifted into the air by the helicopter.

Harry, Natalia, and Woody looked down. No more than twenty feet below them,

Morovich madly piloted his boat into the tiny cove. He hit the wall of rock at over a hundred miles an hour.

The helicopter turned and headed for land. Woody's boat, like the gondola of a huge balloon, floated below it. As they passed over Krokov, the happy trio flashed a victory sign his way.

Krokov kicked off his shoes and tried to float on his back.

At Dodger Stadium in Los Angeles, the crowd was tense. With the bases loaded, the potential leading run was at the plate.

Woody and Natalia sat forward in their seats, waiting for the pitch, along with fifty thousand other fans. Harry sat behind them. He was wearing an earplug and he seemed a bit distracted.

The pitch was delivered; a high fast ball. The batter swung, and a cheer began. The ball soared toward the left field fence, and fifty thousand people sprang to their feet.

By the time the ball disappeared over the fence, the roar had become thunderous.

Woody was jumping up and down. Natalia was clapping her hands.

"A grand slam!" Woody screamed. "A grand slam, Natalia! You brought us luck!"

He turned and kissed her. She slid her arms around him and prolonged the kiss. Then their heads parted and she smiled at him.

"Very nice, Condorman," she said. "We should go to more baseball games."

"Yeah," he said. "Season tickets, first thing tomorrow morning."

Behind them, Harry pushed the plug more tightly into his ear and leaned forward.

"Hey, Natalia!" he said. "Look up. It's my welcome-to-America present to you."

They looked up to see a blimp floating over the stadium. Most of the other fifty thousand people did, too. There was a loud gasp when the message flashed on the side of the airfoil.

WELCOME, NATALIA, TO THE U.S.A.

"Oh, Harry," Natalia said, "it's wonderful."

"Don't mention it," Harry said sheepishly.

Up in the blimp two men looked down through binoculars at the stadium. They were looking specifically at the two people standing in front of Agent Harry Oslo.

Russ Devlin lowered his binoculars and

turned to the other man, who continued to study Woody and Natalia.

"Yes, sir, that's them," Russ said. "But believe me, it's nothing but trouble. If you want my advice—"

"Mr. Devlin," the other man said, still looking through his binoculars, "this assignment is very delicate. It needs to be handled with great finesse."

"That's what I mean, sir. I don't think this man—"

The President of the United States lowered his binoculars and looked at Russ, stopping him in midsentence.

"He got that woman out, didn't he?" the President said. "Do it!"

"Yes, sir, Mr. President. Right away." Russ picked up a microphone and spoke into it. "Set it up, Harry."

Down on the ground, Harry nodded, pulled the plug from his ear, and stuffed it into his shirt pocket. He stepped forward and put one arm around Woody, the other around Natalia. They both smiled at him.

"Woody," Harry said, "you're a good old boy!"

"Uh, thanks, Harry," Woody said, surprised at this sudden outburst of affection.

"I have a suggestion for you," Harry said.

Woody tensed and backed off just a bit. Natalia looked confused.

"Uh, what kind of suggestion, Harry?"

"Oh, nothing too important," Harry said. "Just maybe something you might be able to develop into Condorman's next adventure."

Woody's eyes widened. So did Natalia's. From high above, the President smiled down on his newest agent.